PRESERVATION

PRESERVATION

GHOST SQUADRON BOOK 7

SARAH NOFFKE
MICHAEL ANDERLE

LMBPN

DISRUPTIVE IMAGINATION

LMBPN Publishing
PMB 196, 2540 South Maryland Pkwy
Las Vegas, NV 89109

First US edition, May 2018

PRESERVATION TEAM

INCLUDES

JIT Beta Readers - From all of us, our deepest gratitude!

James Caplan
John Ashmore
Kim Boyer
Micky Cocker
Larry Omans
Peter Manis

*If we missed anyone, **please** let us know!*

Editor
Jen McDonnell

For Lydia. My greatest treasure in the universe.

-Sarah

To Family, Friends and
Those Who Love
To Read.
May We All Enjoy Grace
To Live the Life We Are
Called.

- Michael

Deck 12, Onyx Station, Paladin System

Verdok ran his tongue across the back of his teeth. Having a human mouth always took getting used to. Their teeth were so flat and seemingly useless. At least this body was strong and agile; he couldn't stand impersonating weak humans.

He raised his hand and knocked at the door, listening intently to the shuffling that erupted from the other side. The person he was calling on probably wasn't expecting any visitors.

Multiple locks clinked on the other side before the door slid back, though only as far as the chain would allow. A green eye partly framed by a bushy gray eyebrow blinked back at him. The person startled, jumping back and fumbling with the chain. The door finally flew open, and a woman stood staring, her mouth wide.

"General Reynolds!" she exclaimed, bowing low as she

extended a hand, like she was so surprised she didn't know how to greet the honored guest.

"Annaliese Vincent," Verdok said in a warm voice. "I hope I'm not disturbing you too early."

Annaliese threw her gaze down to the flowery dressing gown she was wearing. She clutched it self-consciously. "Disturbing me? Not at all. But did I miss a note about a meeting?"

Verdok shook his head. "Something has come up, and I'm seeking your help with a project. Can I come in?"

"Of course, General." Annaliese stood back, opening the door wide.

Verdok strode into the spacious apartment, his eyes intent.

"I'm happy to help on a consulting basis, as I've done in the past," Annaliese began.

Verdok slid the briefcase he'd been carrying onto a side table, unbuckling the latches. "Actually, I was hoping you'd take a classified project."

"But I'm retired, and my security access has expired," the old scientist said, hurrying over and looking up at the General.

"I realize that, but…" He fixed a calculating expression on his face before saying, "I suspect that we might have a security breach in R&D. Until I've had time to investigate it further, I need someone I can trust."

"Me?" Annaliese asked, pressing her hands to her chest. "I'm honored. I'll take the project."

Verdok nodded, lifting the case to reveal the two pieces

of the Tangle Thief he'd stolen. "Are you familiar with this piece of technology?"

"That's one of Dr. Hatcherik and Dr. Sung's projects. I read about it," Annaliese said.

"That's correct," Verdok affirmed. "And for obvious reasons, I can't grant you access to the research data. However, I have every confidence that you can fix the device, based on your previous knowledge of the project and your skill set."

"Fix it?" Annaliese asked.

Verdok picked up the two pieces of the Tangle Thief and handed them to the scientist. "Yes, unfortunately they were damaged in transport. I need you to not only repair the devices, but upgrade them."

"Upgrade them?" Apprehension covered the old woman's face. "The project was shut down because it was deemed too dangerous to pursue."

"Correct," Verdok stated. "But things have changed, and we need it operational. This is a matter of galactic security."

Annaliese bristled with fear as she looked the pieces over. "I'm happy to help. This sounds serious."

"It is. I can't give you any more details, but it's crucial that the device works to transport large objects."

"That will take testing."

Verdok nodded. "I assumed as much."

"But what about the tears it leaves behind? The radiation leaks?"

"That's not our concern presently."

Annaliese's eyes widened with alarm.

Verdok coughed discreetly. That's apparently not how the General would respond. "There are other factors at play here that are incredibly important," he said, trying to cover his blunder.

The scientist didn't question this, she simply ran her eyes over the receiver, studying it. Maybe under other circumstance she would, but not when being told this by the General. He was considered the supreme source of truth and to be respected and followed. Verdok had learned this much studying the Federation.

"I also need you to unlink the device so that it can't be connected to any other Tangle Thief clients. Otherwise, our enemies could track down this device with their own."

Annaliese's eyes widened. Verdok really had her attention. "I'll make that my first priority," she said.

"Splendid." Verdok strode back for the door, giving the scientist one last look. "I'll be in touch. For security purposes, you shouldn't attempt to contact me."

She nodded obediently. "Of course. I'll get right to work and wait to hear from you, General Reynolds."

"Very good," Verdok said, a satisfied smile on his face.

McCormick's Pharmacy, Federation Border Station Seven

Lowering the Saverus goggles, Eddie confirmed what they'd suspected with a sharp nod.

Julianna held her gun close to her body, her back pressed to the wall beside the entrance. She cut her eyes to Eddie, who stood in the same position on the other side of the door. With a curt nod, she swung into the mostly empty shop.

"Hands up," she commanded, pointing her weapon at an elderly woman who had been sweeping the floor of a wide aisle stocked with cold remedies.

Eddie directed his gun at a decrepit man sitting behind the counter, leaning over an adding machine.

"What?" the woman said, dropping the broom and hurrying closer to Julianna.

"Stay back," Julianna ordered.

You're holding a senior citizen at gunpoint, Pip scolded in her head. **How low have you sunk?**

She rolled her eyes. *Penrae says that we can't trust them, and fear and surprise, along with keeping them at a distance, could inhibit them from shifting.*

Penrae, the same Saverus who tricked you into jumping into the middle of the enemy's fleet?

I think we can trust that these two are up to something nefarious. The goggles confirmed that they are shapeshifters.

Or they are just two Saverus trying to make an honest living in a world that would distrust them if they showed their real faces.

Would you shush? I need to concentrate.

Yes, I think the evil villain you're after just peed herself.

"What is this about?" the man behind the counter asked, looking between Eddie and Julianna.

"We need to see what's in the back," Julianna stated, her voice clear and deliberate.

"There are only supplies in the back. Nothing of much interest." The old woman dared to take a step toward Julianna.

"Stay back!" Julianna commanded, her gun pointed at the woman's head.

"We're honest business owners," the old man said, his body shaking as he attempted to push up from his stool.

Eddie kept his gun trained on the man. "We know what you are, so stop the bullshit, Saverus."

The woman glanced back at the man. "You must be mistaken. We're human."

Eddie let out a breath, fully annoyed. "You have blue scales and creepy green eyes." He tossed his head in the direction of the man. "And you are yellow with golden eyes."

"Oh, well, since when is it a crime to be an alien?" the man asked, wheezing between each word as he clutched the countertop, inching forward.

"We simply asked to take a look in the back," Julianna stated, pointing her gun at the woman before pivoting it in the man's direction. "You two are going to stay frozen under my supervision while my partner checks it out."

The old man hobbled forward, fumbling with the half-door dividing the counter from the rest of the shop. "That's fine with me. You okay with that, Daisy?"

"I don't see why not," Daisy said as the man continued to attempt to pull open the door.

Why these two picked these feeble bodies, I don't know. Jules lowered her weapon, focusing her gaze on the woman only a few feet away.

"I've got this," Eddie stated, striding for the half-door where the old man seemed to be struggling with the lock.

"This darn thing needs to be greased," the man said, taking a step back so Eddie could unlock it.

"Yeah, it's pretty stubborn," Eddie agreed, his voice returning to his more relaxed tone. These two didn't at all appear to be the criminal Saverus that Penrae had described.

"Mind if I resume sweeping?" the woman asked Julianna, pointing to the broom she'd dropped.

With her curly blue hair and spectacles, she reminded

7

Julianna of her own grandma. Julianna remembered that Granny used to whistle while folding laundry, and often called herself 'an old fart'. The commander found herself smiling at the long-ago memory.

"The afternoon rush is coming, and I'd prefer to get my chores done before then," Daisy said, inclining her head toward the clock on the wall.

Maybe these really are just two, hardworking Saverus, trying to make it in a world that won't accept them for who they are. Shapeshifters aren't considered the most trustworthy, but is it their fault they have such a powerful skill?

"Yeah, go ahead," Julianna stated, stepping on the end of the broom so that its other end popped up.

She leaned forward to retrieve the broom for the old woman and only barely registered movement from the corner of her eyes.

The old woman had vanished, shapeshifting into the hulking figure of a man over seven feet tall. He reached forward, grabbing the broom, and swung it around at Julianna's head. She ducked, then popped back up and brought her arm holding her gun around, slamming it into the massive man's shoulder to no effect. He picked her up by her neck and threw her into a nearby shelf, knocking it over. Julianna's head slammed against the sharp, metal shelf, and her gun flew from her grasp.

From the sound of it, the feeble old man had also shifted and was currently fighting Eddie. Julianna scrambled off the shelf and chanced a look in their direction. The old man had taken the form of a giant Kezzin, and he towered over the captain. He'd apparently fixed his problem with the rusty lock, and threw open the half-door, making Eddie jump back to avoid being hit.

The Kezzin grunted before barreling in Julianna's direction. She kept her shoulders low, darting to the side to get him to chase her, his position matching hers. Tapping the side of his head with her hand, she taunted him in a circle, the two facing off, both looking for the perfect time to attack.

When the huge brute dove for her, Julianna pivoted, putting her back to him before springing backwards into the air. She performed a flip over the imposter, landing hard on his back as he continued forward. Before he knew what was happening, she wrapped her arms around his torso and used her momentum to tumble to the right, pulling the man over her body and down to the ground, pinning his hands. She grabbed his head with both her hands and slammed it into the ground. He fell still at once.

Yeah, so I guess they're probably not as unsuspecting as I first thought, Pip said as Julianna peeled herself off the giant's body.

You think?

A gunshot stole her attention.

Eddie stood, his feet a shoulder-width apart, with his gun pointed straight out in front of him. On the ground, lying lifeless, was the Kezzin. Its body flickered before shifting into the form of a giant snake with golden scales.

"I thought we agreed not to use deadly force if it could be avoided," Julianna said, searching the floor for her gun.

"We did," Eddie said, pointing at the ground behind her. "So what's your excuse?"

She retrieved her pistol from underneath a package of gauze bandages and cast a look at her back. The man she'd fought had been replaced with a blue serpent. "Oops. I guess I don't know my own strength."

"Well, it could still be alive. They do shift back when they're unconscious," Eddie reasoned.

"Good point." Julianna aimed her gun and shot the Saverus in the head. Eddie gave her a questioning look. "What?" she asked, rolling her stiff shoulder. "We can't risk these assholes waking up and starting another fight."

"Good point. Shall we see what's in the back of this seemingly innocent mom and pop shop?" Eddie asked, holding the half-door back for her. It was partially off the hinges, having been punished during the brawl.

Julianna strode behind the counter, gun at the ready, and eyes scanning the back area. She didn't hear noises indicating that anyone else was back there, but she couldn't afford to drop her guard again. Damn Saverus had hit a soft spot, reminding her of her grandmother. She understood exactly why they'd taken on such unsuspecting forms.

A curtain divided the pharmacy from the shop area. It was far less secure than most of the pharmacies on the station, but those tended to have lots of customers; the same didn't seem to be the case for this store.

Julianna and Eddie stealthily moved into the back room, their guns leading their way as they searched the small space. It was no more than fifteen by fifteen feet, and the walls were lined with shelves all holding rows of an identical item.

"Holy fuck!" Eddie exclaimed, looking up to the ceiling.

"Looks like Penrae was telling the truth." Julianna holstered her weapon and picked up one of the vials on the shelf.

There were thousands of small, labeled, stainless steel containers. The one in her hand read:

Race: Human
Gender: Female
Nationality: Asian
Age: 35
Build: Small
Strength: Average
Identity: Unknown

"So this is the Saverus' one-stop shop for getting ahold of new identities," Eddie deduced, picking up a vial and studying the label.

Julianna set down the vial she held. "Apparently, it's one of many shops operating right under the Federation's nose."

"I don't get why they don't just absorb a person's appearance, or whatever it is they do. Why have a shop for specific identities?" Eddie asked.

"I think it's supposed to give them options," Julianna reasoned, picking up another vial.

Eddie held up a bottle. "Hey, how much do you think they charge for these? Do we have a reason for Penrae to look like a Trid?"

Julianna stiffened after reading the label on the vial in

her hand. "I'm guessing this one would cost a bit more than the rest."

"Why is that?" Eddie asked, squinting in her direction.

She turned the label around as she extended her arm, showing him the bottle.

His eyes widened. "'*General Lance Reynolds.*'"

3

Brigg, Ricky Bobby, Tangki System

Eddie held up one of the many vials they'd taken from the pharmacy before they had the place officially shut down. "Hey, maybe we can set up a little date for Lars if you use this one, Penrae."

The serpent crossed through the open door of her cell and read the label. " 'Female Kezzin'? Your brain goes to strange places when there's more pressing matters to attend to, human."

"Tell me about it," Julianna agreed. "Getting him to stay focused is like trying to get a goat to stop chewing on everything."

"I don't get your reference," Penrae stated.

"Nor do I," Eddie said, shaking his head at Julianna before returning his gaze to the Saverus. "And you can call me 'Captain Teach'. I prefer that over 'human'."

"So you've decided to trust me?" Penrae asked, leaning back and studying the pair.

"You were right about the pharmacy, but I'm not sure about trust yet," Julianna allowed.

Penrae nodded, her tongue flicking out of her mouth. "In our training, we are told never to trust anyone. It is a sign of weakness."

Eddie set down the bottle he was studying. "Tell us more about this training."

"I'm not sure how much I can share," Penrae began. "Unveiling any of the secrets of the Saverus order is supposed to cause us great pain. The Elders insist that many a Saverus have died excruciating deaths for doing so."

"Do you think it could be a myth they tell you in order to keep your secrecy?" Julianna asked.

"I'm not sure what to think," Penrae admitted. "I've only ever known the Saverus system of order and government. It is absolute. I've questioned it, but only in my mind."

"Why have you questioned it?" Eddie asked.

A visible shiver transpired down Penrae's body as her eyes grew distant. "The rituals are…complicated, to say the least, and I daresay a bit unorthodox."

"Rituals?" Julianna questioned.

"The Saverus…Well, I'm not sure how much to say…"

"Have you felt any pain from what you've told us so far?" Eddie asked.

"Well, no, but—" Penrae admitted.

"Start with something small," Julianna suggested.

The Saverus' eyes shifted nervously. "We can hold up to six identities at a time and shift into them at will," she began, growing more confident as she spoke.

"But the identities in the bank are different, aren't they?" Julianna asked.

Penrae nodded. "We can carry the vials on us and change into them as needed. It's insurance, in case we need a different appearance."

"Or a specific one, in the case of General Reynolds," Eddie guessed.

"That's correct," Penrae confirmed, swaying slightly, lost in thought. "As I've hinted at, we only need to be in close proximity to borrow an identity, but it isn't always an option for us to get close to someone. That's another reason for the vials."

"Any pain or discomfort yet?" Julianna asked.

Penrae checked over her body, like looking for a physical scar. "No, not at all."

"I really think that you've been brainwashed," Julianna reasoned.

"It's actually brilliant," Eddie argued. "The only way to test that is with disobedience, which I'm sure no one would want to chance."

"We're told all of this so early on that it's hard to fight it," Penrae stated. Julianna didn't know what the Saverus was thinking about, but she could see her eyes shifting in intensity. "That's why we went along with the sacrificial practices, and why we were pushed off of Savern."

"Penrae?" Julianna asked, leaning down to look up into the serpent's eyes. "Are you all right?"

Slowly she nodded. "That's the thing, I'm fine. But after that admission, I didn't expect to be."

"Is how you were run off your home planet a big secret?" Eddie asked.

"Yes, but I decided to tell you because I'd rather be struck down now by the gods than continue to live with the secrets that the Elders told me that I've questioned all my life," Penrae admitted.

Eddie couldn't fathom questioning his own cultural framework—of course, he'd never been given reason to distrust the Federation or those who raised him. "Go on then," he encouraged. "Let it all out."

Penrae took a deep breath. "Many centuries ago, species of all types came to live on Savern, attracted by its beautiful landscape and warm temperature," she began, slithering back and forth as she spoke. "With others to witness the Saverus' ways, our species was put under fire. The other aliens condemned our ancestors, claimed that our rituals were wrong, that we told our children lies. That sacrificing our own kind to the gods was horribly unjust."

Julianna gasped, interrupting.

"I know...or at least, I'm starting to understand," Penrae assured her. "There was a bloody battle over the difference in our ideals, and the Saverus were defeated. Our ancestors disappeared and sought to cover up any trace that our race had ever lived. From then forward, we lived in secret, not telling anyone that we were shapeshifters, still dwelling in space and prowling among civilizations."

"And over time, the race became a myth," Eddie finished for her, in awe that they'd been able to accomplish such a task.

"It wasn't hard, since we can blend in so easily," Penrae said. "We were able to create a secret infrastructure to support our kind."

"Like the pharmacy," Julianna guessed.

Penrae nodded. "And we stole the riches of others to build our own fortune."

"Which is how the Saverus obtained a fleet that makes me wet myself," Eddie stated, remembering the vast force they'd accidentally dropped into that included several large battle cruisers.

"Yes, and I suspect that they've already changed locations," Penrae said.

"They have," Julianna confirmed.

"So the Saverus have been biding their time for all these years. Why come out now and go after the Tangle Thief? What's the end goal?" Eddie asked.

Penrae hesitated, still afraid her next words would scorch her insides. "Isn't it obvious?" she asked after a moment.

"I'm afraid it isn't," Eddie said.

Penrae didn't say anything, apprehension boiling in her eyes.

"So far, nothing you've said has harmed you," Julianna reasoned. "You've been brainwashed and abused, but it was all lies. If you help us, we will do what your Elders never did. We'll empower you and trust you."

Penrae straightened, seeming to find a new confidence. "The Saverus want the Tangle Thief so they can steal back the home planet."

"What?" Julianna asked, alarm flaring in her voice. "But they'll create a tear in the galaxy that could destroy it."

Penrae nodded. "The Elders don't care. They only care about themselves. They want to take Savern back for good."

4

Hatch's Lab, *Ricky Bobby*, Tangki System

"So I tell the guy, 'if you're so sure, why don't we throw down right here and now?'" Pip boasted over the speaker.

Hatch lifted his eyes from the client on the workstation, shaking his head at Knox. "That never happened."

"It's more of a hypothetical," Pip said defensively. "If someone threw some shade on me, I'd open up a can of whoop ass."

Knox burst out laughing, unable to control himself.

Hatch puffed out his cheeks, not looking impressed. "I didn't understand a word you just said."

"When are we going to work on getting Pip a body?" Knox asked him.

"One with pecs," Pips added.

Hatch actually smiled at this. "It's definitely on the long list of projects. But first, I'm working on integrating you into Teach and establishing control over muscle function."

"I can already regulate Julianna's breathing, temperature and pain receptors. How difficult is it to give me the ability to control their bodies?" Pip asked.

"In theory, it shouldn't be difficult at all, but a bad connection could have serious repercussions for the captain," Knox explained, having done much of the research.

The head mechanic agreed with a nod. "Which for me isn't a deterrent. The wait is mostly about me finding time for the project and determining a new way to bind you into their human form. Maybe after we finish up with this client I'll be able to look into it."

Knox attached a series of wires to the Tangle Thief, using precision to ensure the connections were tight. He hadn't returned to his old self since losing the other pieces of the device, but Hatch thought it was because Knox was evolving, becoming something new based on his experiences in the junkyard.

"I'm still not getting a reading on a compatible device," Hatch reported, staring at a screen beside his workstation.

"Which means?" Knox asked.

"It *could* mean that the other pieces of the Tangle Thief are destroyed," he proposed hopefully.

"Or that they've simply been disconnected so that we can't track them down," Pip added.

Knox's shoulders slumped slightly, to Hatch's dismay.

"I was getting to that," Hatch grumbled, irritated with the AI's lack of decorum.

In other matters, he didn't mind Pip's bluntness so much…but Knox needed them to track down the Tangle Thief. It was part of his redemption.

"Good morning," Liesel chirped, striding into the lab, carrying a small white box and searching the workspace. In the front pocket of her overalls sat Sebastian, his head and tail poking out of either end. "Is Harley in here?"

"He is not," Hatch said, his attention back on the client. "I don't allow the dog in here. This is a mechanic's lab, not a kennel."

"Since the upgrade, he's less of a dog and more of a team member," Knox argued.

Hatch cut his eyes at him, earning a look of apology. "He still sheds and gets into stuff."

"I was only asking because Sebastian still has issues after being chased," Liesel explained.

"He wasn't the one that got stuck in a vent shaft and nearly died," Pip accused.

Liesel smiled sensitively. "Yes, but Sebastian is still dealing with trauma, not to mention guilt over what happened to Harley."

"Can we get a little therapy for the ferret with PTSD?" Pip joked.

Liesel pulled the ferret from her pocket and placed him on her shoulder. He crawled down her back and all the way to the floor, scurrying for the back of the lab.

"Don't touch anything," Hatch warned, wagging a tentacle menacingly in the air at the animal.

Liesel set the white paper box on a nearby workstation. "I brought you all breakfast; I know you've been working nonstop on the client."

"Wakey, wakey, eggs and bakey!" Pip said with enthusiasm.

Liesel blew a breath upward, knocking her bangs off her forehead. "I'm a vegan, you know that."

"Oh." Pip sounded deflated. "Wakey, wakey, veggies and sadness."

Liesel shook her head good naturedly at the joke. "Pip, I thought you were all for a vegan diet."

"That's before I had the prospect of a body," Pip stated. "The captain is going to eat all sorts of cheesy foods once we're paired. The captain is going to eat all sorts of cheesy foods when I take over. Mozzarella sticks, nachos, macaroni and cheese, pizza, quesadillas, cheesecake—"

"We get the point," Hatch cut the excited AI off.

"Well, I made you all vegan donuts," Liesel said with a wide smile. Automotive wire was wrapped around her blonde pigtails, its frayed ends sticking up.

"Uhhh…Thanks, but I'm not hungry." Knox dropped his gaze, suddenly looking very busy.

"And I don't eat vegetables," Hatch stated blankly. "If you have any crab cakes, I'll take those."

"I'm afraid I don't," Liesel said, pushing the box farther onto the workstation. "Well, I'll leave these in case you all change your mind. I swear they taste like real donuts."

"Anytime you have to describe your food as tasting like the real thing, it's considered fake and therefore not as good," Hatch reasoned.

Liesel laughed. "As soon as I said that, I knew you'd chide me for it."

"What is in these not-real donuts?" Pip asked. "I'm thinking about going into baking when I have a body."

Knox darted his eyes up to meet Hatch's. "Can you picture the captain wearing an apron?"

"Actually, that reminds me, Pip," Hatch said, combing a tentacle over his wobbly chin. "I have a proposition for you and Teach's body."

"I'm listening." Pip sounded curious.

Hatch looked over his shoulder at Liesel. "We'll discuss it later. Go on then, about the donuts," he said, quickly diverting the conversation. The fewer people he let in on his cruel joke, the better.

Liesel tucked a stray piece of hair behind her ear. "Well, the recipe is fairly easy. It calls for aquafaba, almond milk, almond flour—"

"What's aquafaba?" Knox asked.

"Oh, it's the liquid in canned beans," Liesel explained.

"Yum!" Pip chirped sarcastically.

Knox eyed the box of pastries, his face restrained. "That's a creative use for the substance."

"Aquafaba is used in place of egg as the binding agent," Liesel stated.

Hatch jerked his head up. "That's it!"

Knox and Liesel exchanged curious expressions.

"Okay, I'll bite," Pip finally said, breaking the strange silence. "What's it?"

"I've figured out how I'll bind you, Pip, into Teach," Hatch said, his voice vibrating with excitement. He loved moments of scientific revelation, and that inspiration could come from anywhere.

"With an egg substitute?" Pip asked.

Hatch shook his head, bustling over to his computer

station. "I've got to change the binding agent. It needs to be compatible, similar to the one we used for installing you in Julianna, but it will have a different chemical makeup."

"So you're using bean juice, in essence," Knox said, his tone growing with enthusiasm as he processed the theory and realized how genius it was.

"Exactly!" Hatch typed furiously, recording his ideas.

"And then the captain and I will bind and make a vegan donut!" Pip said victoriously.

5

Jack Renfro's Office, *Ricky Bobby*, Tangki System

Jack eyed the green smoothie in his hands like it was toxic waste.

"What is that?" Eddie asked, playing with one of the many "toys" Jack displayed on the far wall, most of them related to science or mathematics.

"It's a wheatgrass shake." Jack took a deep breath, held his nose and took a sip.

"Why are you forcing yourself to drink that?" Julianna asked.

Coming up for air, Jack wiped his mouth of the sludge. "Because it's good for me."

Eddie pulled back one of the balls hanging from the pendulum of the Newton's cradle before releasing it. He watched the opposite ball swing, having been displaced by the motion. "If you want to live an extra few hundred years, why don't you take a nap in a Pod-doc instead of forcing yourself to drink slime?"

Jack nodded, setting the drink down and pushing it away. "Yeah, I get where Liesel is coming from with this conscious living approach, but I'm not sure if the diet is for me."

"I think the beauty of a good relationship is that you don't have to become like each other to be together," Julianna stated.

Eddie and Jack both gave her quizzical expressions, the only sound in the room being the clicking of the pendulum balls.

"What?" Julianna asked.

Eddie pointed to Harley, who sat stoically beside Julianna. He looked regal with his shiny coat and sharp gaze. "That dog has had an effect on you."

Julianna ignored this with a shake of her head. "Jack, before you tried poisoning yourself with nutrients, you mentioned something about new weapons." The excitement was palpable in her voice.

Jack popped up to a standing position, his hands clasping behind his back, his eyes pinned on his desk. This was quickly becoming known as 'Jack's briefing stance'. "Have you heard of the Nihilist organization?"

"No, but I already don't like them," Eddie stated. "I'm guessing they aren't known for holding peace rallies."

Jack shook his head. "No, quite the opposite. The anti-government organization is responsible for a handful of bombing attempts on Onyx Station and Federation Border Station 7."

"Where do we find them and how do we take them out?" Eddie asked, striding over to Jack's desk and taking a seat. Julianna never sat down when in Jack's office, choosing rather to stand beside the chair. She rarely sat, actually.

"We got a tip that they are planning another bombing on Onyx," Jack began. "I have Chester hacking their communications to find more details."

"So we need to step in and stop them on Onyx station," Julianna stated.

Jack shook his head. "I have Chester working overtime to find the location of their current base. I thought we could kill two birds with one stone."

Eddie leaned forward. "Not sure why you're slaughtering birds when terrorists should be our focus, but you've got my attention."

"I'd read that Lieutenant Fletcher has had a few run-ins with the Nihilist organization," Jack explained. "When I questioned him on it, he said they'd slipped by his efforts more than a few times. Apparently, they have an arsenal of impressive weapons, which always give them the advantage."

"Impressive weapons?" Julianna asked. "Now *I'm* paying attention."

Jack released one of his easy grins. "I thought that might get you. Ghost Squadron has needed better guns for quite some time. If Chester can track down Nihilist headquarters, you can surprise them there. We stop the bombing, and you confiscate their arsenal."

"Meanwhile, none of the space stations know there was ever a threat," Julianna stated.

Eddie smiled wide. "And continue to sleep peacefully in their beds."

6

Hatch's Lab, *Ricky Bobby*, Tangki System

Julianna tapped her foot, her anxiety seeking to bound out of her chest.

Your heart rate is elevated, Pip observed.

Shouldn't you be concentrating or chanting or something, she retorted, irritation heavy in her tone.

Hatch told me to sit back and relax while he does all the work.

Ha-ha, Julianna spat with zero humor. She eyed the table on the far side of the room where Eddie was stretched out. He reminded her more of an aircraft getting an upgrade than a human undergoing a complicated procedure.

Try petting Harley's head, Pip suggested. **That has shown to increase serotonin levels.**

Julianna dropped her eyes to the dog stationed at her side. *I'm good.*

I've sifted through many of your memories and can't locate the one that produced your fear of dogs.

I don't fear Harley.

You don't *anymore*, but originally his presence elevated your blood pressure. Now it does quite the opposite.

I'm not the touchy-feely type. He understands that.

Does he? Pip questioned. Before Julianna could tell him where to stick his loaded question, he said, **I must be off. The captain is calling me.**

Fuck my life, Julianna thought, pressing her eyes closed.

I heard that, Pip chimed before falling completely silent. Julianna felt the absence that she attributed to Pip being busy, usually in Hatch's lab. Now that absence would be because Pip was hanging out in Eddie's head, discussing who knows what.

Julianna turned, putting her back to the far side of the room and pretending to study a workstation filled with devices.

Is everything okay? Harley asked.

Yeah, it's fine...well, actually I think it's as far from fine as possible.

Do you want to talk about it? Harley offered.

Julianna shook her head, but then her words betrayed her.

I think I do, she heard herself say.

Eddie sat up before he was ordered to do so, which earned him a contemptuous stare from Hatch.

"Dammit, Teach," Hatch bellowed. "Are you trying to ruin everything?"

"What if I told you it wasn't my fault?" Eddie asked.

Hatch's scowl fell away. "Was it not your fault? Did Pip make you sit up?"

Eddie shook his head. "Nah, I have to take full blame. I got up of my own accord."

Hatch grunted with frustration. "Figures. You literally can't follow directions to save your own life."

"How do we know if it worked?" Eddie asked.

Scanning a computer screen, Hatch said, "Well, how do you feel? Can you hear Pip in your head?"

Eddie stared without seeing, trying to determine if he felt changed. "Does he sound different than my own thoughts?" he asked.

Hatch waved Julianna over with a tentacle. She appeared more than reluctant to come forward. "Julie, can you explain the difference between Pip's voice and your thoughts?"

Julianna slid her hands into her pockets, a tense expression on her face. "You'll know the difference."

Hatch shrugged, only partially satisfied with her inadequate answer. "There you go. Try talking to him. The connection appears to be made, but it might still be in transition."

Pip, are you there? Eddie asked, feeling silly talking to himself.

Nothing.

Eddie pursed his lips, scanning his body, like expecting it to look different. *Hey, buddy, are you there yet?* he tried again.

Hey, buddy, are you there yet, a voice echoed in his mind.

That's strange, Eddie thought.

That's strange, the voice repeated.

Pip, is that you repeating what I say?

Pip, is that you repeating what I say, Pip said, a hint of a laughter in his voice.

Eddie smiled. "I think we have a clear connection."

"You *think?*" Hatch asked, not at all sounding impressed with the less than definitive response.

"Well, Pip appears to be repeating everything I say, but I think that's him," Eddie said.

Julianna shook her head. "That's him."

"We need to determine if he has control over your body," Hatch stated. "In most instances, you'll have to relinquish control to him. I made it so he didn't have free reign over your body, although if you're not paying attention, he might be able to take over."

"That sounds troublesome," Eddie said with a laugh. *How bad can it be, having an AI who has access to my body? What's the worst we could do?*

"You've been warned," Hatch stated. "Go ahead and relax and try to give him control."

Eddie drew in a deep breath and let it out slowly. *Pip?*

Yes, Eddie? he answered.

Oh, good, you're talking to me finally.

The experience of having something…well, some*one* in

his mind was incredibly surreal. *This will take some getting used to.*

For now I'm talking to you. I'm great at giving Julianna the cold shoulder, Pip said playfully.

Ha-ha. I can't wait for all the games.

I'm a player, what can I say.

Let's be serious for a moment. Can you control my body? Eddie asked.

Yes, I believe so.

Eddie smiled. "He says he has control."

Hatch let out an annoyed sigh. "I work in the world of provable facts. Will you please have him show us?"

Eddie's hand lifted without his consent and waved at them.

"There you go," he said, watching his hand being waved as if by a puppeteer holding invisible strings.

Knox laughed.

"Are you serious?" Hatch nearly yelled, his face brightening with pink.

"What?" Eddie asked, confused.

"How do we know that's Pip waving your hand and not you?" Julianna asked.

"I didn't do it," Eddie explained.

"We need a better way of testing this." Hatch rotated in the direction of his computer station, reviewing data as it scrolled on the screen.

"Maybe we give him a sedative?" Knox offered. "Pip is supposed to be able to control the captain's body even if he's unconscious, right?"

"Although that's an excellent suggestion, I think there's

an easier way," Hatch said, peering deep into Eddie's eyes like he was trying to find the AI inside of him.

What's he talking about? Do you know? Eddie asked Pip.

I sure do, Pip answered.

What is it?

You're not going to like it.

Eddie laughed. *Are you going to make me stand on my head?*

"Pip," Hatch interrupted. "Remember what we discussed? You want me to fulfill my end of the bargain, you've got to fulfill yours."

What does he mean? Eddie asked.

Sorry about this, captain.

Before Eddie could reply, his own hand shot up and slapped himself across the cheek. The assault was so hard it whipped his face to the side.

Like struck by a close friend, Eddie blinked in disbelief for a few seconds, the whole room having fallen silent.

"And there it is!" Hatch cheered. "The moment I've been waiting for. There's conclusive proof that Pip is controlling Teach's body."

Eddie shut down any access Pip had over him. *I can't believe you slapped me.*

I believe *you* slapped you, Pip said, his tone sassy.

Wasn't there another way?

That's what Hatch told me to do.

Eddie shot an accusatory look at the mechanic. "You told him to slap me?"

"That I did," Hatch sang, turning and waddling for the

other side of the lab. "Keep up your side of the bargain, I'll keep up mine, Pip."

"What bargain?" Eddie asked, jumping off the lab table. *What is he talking about, Pip?*

We made a deal, Pip answered.

What kind of deal?

It's a secret.

Eddie grunted, catching Julianna's amused expression. "I've been set up," he told her.

She nodded, not at all looking surprised. "Which is exactly why I wasn't dumb enough to allow that psychotic AI to have control over my body."

Pardon me, Captain, Pip said. **I'll be right back. I've got to go crazy on someone's ass.**

7

Intelligence Center, *Ricky Bobby*, Tangki System

A loud voice boomed from the Intelligence Center when Julianna and Eddie rounded into the space. Julianna had half expected to find a large man with a round stomach, smoking a pipe. Instead, only Chester and Marilla were in the large work area. A voice with a thick British accent boomed over the surround sound speakers, his articulation impressive and tone captivating.

Chester had his head reclined and his eyes closed as he listened to the audiobook, which Julianna recognized as a Sherlock Holmes novel. Marilla, on the other hand, was engrossed in her work, not even seeming to notice the theatrical audio playing overhead.

"Ricky Bobby, would you pause Chester's book?" Julianna asked.

The AI didn't even respond, only halted the audio, making the room fall silent. Chester cracked one eye open, his lazy gaze finding the captain and commander at once.

"It is ever a wonder that no one besides you two want to work in here," Eddie said, twisting his finger in his ear and trying to dispel the ringing from the loud voice.

"I'm not an easy person to share a space with," Chester admitted, opening his eyes and sitting up all the way. "I make no secret of the fact."

"Marilla, how do you put up with this guy?" Eddie asked, throwing a thumb in the hacker's direction.

"I have the ability to tune out all unnecessary noise and focus despite my surroundings," Marilla said in a monotone voice, her eyes never leaving her computer screen.

"That proves there's someone for everyone," Eddie sang, pulling out a rolling chair and taking a seat.

The captain doesn't think that anyone will ever put up with his annoying habits, Pip informed Julianna.

He's probably right, she responded, her tone neutral.

Interested to hear about some of those habits? I've made a list of them.

Eddie had no idea what he was getting himself into when he invited you into his head. And no, I don't care to hear about his annoying habits.

Yeah, he wasn't interested in hearing the list of yours either.

Julianna ignored Pip, pretending to pay attention to the current conversation between Eddie and Chester.

Or maybe the captain didn't have the time to hear your list. It's rather long.

You're wicked, goat-licker.

Name calling, I'll add that to the list.

Why don't you. I'm kind of busy right now. Make yourself scarce.

Eddie and Chester had fallen into an easy conversation about the *Hound of Baskerville*, chatting excitedly about their favorite parts.

"Can we table this discussion?" Julianna interrupted, looking directly at Chester. "We need to find out what you discovered about the Nihilist organization."

Eddie's exuberant expression dropped, replaced with a more acceptable one. "That's right. But hook me up with this audio when you have a chance, Chester. My eyes are too tired to read at night."

"Teach, when did you take up classic literature?" Julianna asked.

Eddie looked up at her. "Since Chester gave me a reading list."

Julianna gave Chester a sideways expression full of disbelief. "I took you as more of a science fiction reader."

Chester pointed at Marilla without looking at her. "That's all Marilla. She's read everything of Asimov's."

"Your mind is blown, isn't it, Jules?" Eddie asked.

She shook her head. "I'll admit, you two are breaking stereotypes."

"When it comes to films, we are more predictable," Chester admitted. "I prefer action, and Mar watches mostly foreign films."

Julianna's brow wrinkled. "We're in space, crossing between solar systems on a regular basis. What exactly is considered 'foreign'?"

"Stuff with subtitles," Chester said, like this should have

been obvious. He bolted forward in his seat, typing on a keyboard. "But you came to learn about evil terrorists, not to discuss the post-classic era crossover of noir into science fiction."

"You didn't make a lot of friends in school, did you?" Eddie asked Chester lightly.

"Not a single one," the hacker said with a laugh before hitting a final key, his bright eyes darting to the largest monitor. An aerial image of a giant compound guarded by a tall fence illuminated the screen. "I present to you the Nihilist compound, also affectionately nicknamed by its leaders as 'the Jungle'."

Julianna rolled her eyes. "My disdain is growing for this group. A bunch of guerillas, hanging out in 'the jungle'."

Chester fired a finger gun at her. "Bingo, Commander."

"How did you find all this out?" Eddie asked.

"I established contact by selling them a bunch of nukes," he answered.

"Which they will be expecting," Julianna guessed.

"Yes," he confirmed. "Once I established contact, I was able to hack into their network and learn that they plan on bombing Onyx Station in two days."

"Over my dead body," Eddie argued.

"Which is why I set up for the nuke exchange to happen the day before," Chester countered triumphantly.

Eddie beamed, his eyes buzzing with excitement. "Great! So Jules and I take them their supposed nuke, instead giving them a rude awakening. I like it."

"That would have worked, but the leader, Conway, wouldn't go for a delivery. There's a rendezvous spot where they'll pick up the nuke. They'll transfer half the funds for the weapon when I deliver it, and the other half once they have it securely back at the Jungle."

"Then scrap all this," Julianna stated. "We'll invade the headquarters and be done with it."

Chester's eyes narrowed, a skeptical expression on his face. "That would be a good solution, except that the Nihilists have much better weapons than you do. It would be like storming one of the Federation's strongholds. You might be enhanced, but you can still get shot in the head."

"So what are you proposing?" Eddie asked.

"I looked the plan over with Hatch, and we both agreed this was the best option." Chester typed several commands on his keyboard, bringing up an image of a fifty-five-ton missile. "I'm going to deliver them this."

Marilla's chin whipped up, her eyes wide. The crazy scheme had made it through her selective hearing.

"*You?*" Eddie asked. "Why would you deliver the weapon? Why not us?"

Chester let out an exaggerated sigh. "Because then you can't be hiding inside the missile."

"Uhhh...riiiiiight," Eddie said, drawing out the word.

"We have an intercontinental ballistic missile sitting around for us to deliver?" Julianna asked.

"Hatch says that if he skips lunch, we will," Chester stated.

"And we're going to hide in this missile?" Eddie asked.

"Think about it," Chester implored. "You could infiltrate the compound and most likely get caught—I've done searches on the security protocols for the Jungle, and breaking in there isn't easy. *Or* I can sell them a fake nuke, you could stow away inside it, and once you're behind the gates, make your move."

"What's the catch?" Julianna asked, immediately skeptical.

"Right, you caught me," he admitted. "Since testing the weapon is impossible in the field, Conway is going to have his scientists evaluate the nuke once it is transferred. So you have a tiny, miniscule window to get out of the nuke and take control of the compound before they find you."

Eddie gave Julianna a measured look. "It would be much better to be in place and ready to kick ass than to have the door opened on us."

"Is there room for Fletcher's team inside the missile shell?" Julianna asked, pointing to the screen. The missile was loaded on an eighteen-wheeled vehicle, comprising most of its trailer.

"And then some," Chester sang.

"And you're delivering the weapon?" Marilla asked, apprehension dripping in her tone.

Chester's eyes fell, the light in them dimming slightly. "The only way I could make the deal with Conway was over a video conference. He insisted I be a part of the exchange, since he knows what I look like. If I don't show up, he's going to be immediately suspicious."

"What if we hadn't gone for your idea?" Eddie asked.

He huffed. "It's kind of a brilliant plan. I knew you'd like it."

"We didn't ask for you to strategize our access into the

Jungle, though," Julianna said, unable to keep the disapproval out of her voice.

"No, I realize I overstepped my bounds," Chester stated. "But when I was told to track down the compound, one thing led to another. You still have to figure out the strategy once you spill out of that missile, so...good luck with that."

Marilla crossed her arms in front of her chest, her eyes hard. "I don't like it."

"There is a lot that could go wrong," Eddie agreed.

"And yet," Ricky Bobby chimed in overhead, "when I run different simulations, this scenario has the least amount of potential threats. Storming the place, or even trying to sneak in by disabling the security, led to absolute annihilation of the squad."

Julianna gave Eddie a long, weighted look.

"Eddie, what do you—"

He thinks we ought to do it, Pip cut in.

Julianna gritted her teeth and shook her head.

"Did Pip just tell you I think it's a good idea?" Eddie asked and then grunted. "Never mind."

Isn't it wonderful! I've streamlined your conversations. Pip sounded entirely too proud of himself.

Please tell me you're going to get tired of this, Julianna pleaded.

Yes, especially if the captain is serious about the threats he just made to me.

Julianna smiled at Eddie. Pip might think he had the upper hand, but he couldn't keep playing them against each other.

8

Loading Dock, *Ricky Bobby*, Tangki System

"Whoa," Eddie exclaimed when he rounded the corner. The missile was larger than he'd expected, taking up a huge portion of the loading dock. "You built that?" he asked Hatch.

"It's only the case," Hatch said. "It's not like there's actual nuclear technology inside of it."

Fletcher's team filed out of the front end of the missile, one after another, like clowns from a car at the circus.

"Is your team ready?" Julianna asked the lieutenant.

"Yes, we've run through the mission a dozen times," Fletcher answered, clapping his hands together and rubbing them eagerly. "We're ready to go."

Eddie wasn't sure if it was the nerves connected to the mission, but Fletcher seemed a bit too excited for this, if that was possible.

Julianna has the same opinion, Pip informed him.

Eddie cut his eyes to Julianna, a knowing expression in her gaze.

Maybe there is something good about you sharing a place in both our heads, Eddie stated.

There's a lot of good things. Just you wait. Pip's tone sounded ominous.

The crew began to load the missile into one of the two transport ships they'd take to Kezza, where the Jungle was located. One ship for the missile and team, and the other for the store of weapons they hoped to take from the Nihilists. If this worked out, they'd disband a corrupt organization *and* have state-of-the-art weapons. Eddie loved pirating supplies from the enemy. It was a win-win.

Hatch's tentacle stretched through the air, waving a key in front of Eddie's face. "Here, take this."

"What's it for?" Eddie asked.

"You need to secure an eighteen-wheeler on Kezza to transport the missile," Hatch informed him.

"Aw, and you've already gotten me the key. Sweet," Eddie guessed, taking it from Hatch's tentacle.

"No, that's to your ride to the semi," Hatch said, bustling around. "Pip knows the details."

"Why don't *I* know the details?" Eddie asked, irritated.

"Because you're an idiot who's on a need-to-know basis," Hatch mumbled.

Eddie gave Julianna a questioning look.

"What about me, Hatch?" Julianna asked.

"Don't you worry, Julie," Hatch said, his tone softer. "I've got you covered."

Julianna shrugged, her worry disappearing from her expression.

What's going on, Pip? Eddie asked him.

Nothing much, just playing Minecraft.

I meant what's going on between you and Hatch?

Oh, that? It's nothing. Just boring logistics. Silly transportation details.

Sounds like I should be worried.

Don't you trust me, Ed?

Don't call me that.

Running footsteps stole Eddie's attention, and he and Julianna turned to find Chester jogging in their direction.

"I'm here!" Chester said, shoving a laptop into his backpack.

"What's that for?" Julianna asked, indicating the bag.

"Figured that I could communicate with you all over the comms once you're in place," he answered, panting. "If I'm in close proximity, I'll be able to hack into the Jungle's security mainframe and bypass some of their protocols."

"You keep making our jobs easier," Eddie said with a whistle.

"All right, people, look alive," Julianna commanded, clapping her hands together. "Let's load up and move out."

Planet Kezza, Tangki System

The transport ship set down in a wide valley that gave coverage from spying eyes. Eddie had spent the ride to Kezza watching Fletcher nervously fidget. Something had the XO more on edge than usual, and it was hard for the captain to believe it was only the high stakes. Yes, they would be battling their way out of a large compound where the terrorists held better weapons than them. However, it was impossible that these anarchists were better trained, even if they had railguns.

Julianna gave Eddie a curious look as they disembarked.

"Fletcher caught your eyes too, I heard," he said from the corner of his mouth.

"Yeah, but I can't figure it out," she said, casting her eyes over her shoulder. "And there are others I'm more concerned about."

Chester trotted down the ramp behind them, a little ways off. He wasn't used to battle, but he'd also never let them down. He was a guy who knew how to rise to the occasion.

Eddie halted when they were on the ground, and waited for the hacker to join them. "You ready for this?"

Chester choked on the first part of his answer. "Yeah." He cleared his throat. "I was born ready."

"All right," Julianna exhaled, looking around. "Where's the transport to the semi that Hatch promised?"

Jules and Edward, it's right behind you, Pip stated in both of their heads.

They turned in unison to see a shiny, red 1969 Corvette Stingray being pushed down the ramp of the transport ship.

"No fucking way!" Eddie yelled. "Hatch is going to let us drive this?"

Correction, Captain, Pip said. **Hatch is going to let *me* drive this. It's part of our bargain.**

Chester retrieved his ringing phone from his pocket and tapped the screen. "Hey, doc! We made it."

"About time," Hatch's voice sounded over the speaker. "Turn me around so I can see Teach."

Chester complied, facing the screen in Eddie's direction. Hatch stared back from the small screen.

"Okay, Pip," Hatch said. "Ready to pony up on your end of the deal?"

What's he talking about? Eddie asked.

Remember how he said that you had to relinquish control for me to move your body? Pip asked.

Yeeeeeees, Eddie said, drawing out the word.

He lied.

Both Eddie's hands rose, the right slapping him on one cheek and then the other, repeatedly.

A booming laugh echoed from the phone as Hatch doubled over. "Oh, damn, Captain," Hatch said through a fit of laughter. "Why are you hitting yourself?"

Julianna and Chester joined in, and thankfully the torture stopped after a few seconds.

When Hatch had regained his composure, he said, "Good job, Pip. You have my blessing."

"Wait, Pip makes a mockery of me, and he gets to drive the Stingray?" Eddie asked, slightly amused.

"That's right," Hatch stated. "But after the drive, Pip, remember the rule."

Eddie tensed. "What rule?" he asked.

"No more pranks," Hatch said, his tone suddenly serious. "I appreciate you being a good sport about this, Captain. But going forward, Pip isn't to take control of your body without your consent unless it is to save your life."

Eddie laughed. "I can't believe you two made this deal." He realized he should have been offended, but it was pretty cleverly executed.

It was worth it, Pip said, making Eddie hold up the keys and shake them in the air. **I'm ready to enjoy my first cruise on the open road.**

Eddie couldn't help but smile. If anyone deserved this, it was the AI.

"Be careful with her, Pip," Hatch warned. "I'd tell you not to allow Teach to touch the car, but that would be impossible."

The Stingray left Chester in its dust after dropping him off at the semi. There was no way the big truck could keep up with the sports car, the way Pip was driving.

Pip, using Eddie's body, shifted gears, peeling around the dusty roads that snaked through the mountains.

Are you enjoying yourself? Eddie asked the AI.

Hell yeah, I am.

On the straightaway, Pip cranked the speedometer up to ninety miles per hour.

I think you're going a bit fast there, buddy.

I think you're jealous.

It was strange for Eddie to have his hands on the wheel yet not be in control. It surprised him, the way Pip used his hands —not always gripping the shifter, like he would—and sat differently than he was accustomed. Although he could feel his body, he was a mere observer of the whole experience.

You know who is probably jealous ? Jules.

Pip turned Eddie's head and looked at the bucket seat where Chester had ridden on the way to the eighteen-wheeler.

Yeah, I definitely wish she were here. She'd rag me about burning out the clutch when I first took off, Pip said a longing in his voice.

She never lets me get away with anything. She always keeps me on my toes, Eddie related.

A good woman teases you over your faults, while cataloging your strengths and filing them away, remembered for all of time.

Damn, that's some poetry, Pip.

In other news, hold onto your ass. Pip accelerated, making the needle teeter close to one hundred.

I would, but you kind of own it right now.

Damn straight I do. Don't you forget it.

They were quickly approaching the area where the ships and crew were located, ready to load the missile silo onto the semi when Chester arrived. The warhead lay on its side in the center of the clearing.

Hey what you got planned? Eddie asked, feeling tense but unable to show it.

Relax. I got this, Pip responded, slowing, but not

enough. They were quickly approaching the fake, giant nuke.

Pip pushed in the clutch while slamming on the brakes. He jerked up the parking brake and whipped the wheel around, leaving rubber on the road as the tires squealed. The car's rear end spun in a one-eighty. It would have been a perfect move, except for the bumper grazing against the missiles outer skin at the last moment, making an awful screeching noise. Even though Eddie's foot was pressed firmly on the brake, the car continued to drift, raking against the silo until it finally came to an abrupt halt.

Eddie's hand gripped the Corvette's steering wheel, and his face was pink with embarrassment. Julianna stepped out of the crowd of soldiers and strolled over, a calm expression on her face. She eyed the bumper crunched up against the missile silo as she sauntered up to the car, and bent down, setting her arms on the open window of the convertible.

"I hope you enjoyed your ride, Pip, because Hatch is going to murder you," she said casually, her voice almost sweet.

Pip released his control over Eddie's body, and retreated into his mind. His time in the spotlight had been absolutely diminished by the scratching of the car.

Eddie hopped out of the Corvette, gauging the damage. "Let's be glad that's not an active missile."

"And hope that the Nihilists don't mind a bit of red paint on their warhead," Julianna added.

9

Planet Kezza, Tangki System

"Are you ready for this?" Nona asked Fletcher, pulling her eyes away from the missile as it was loaded onto the bed of the eighteen-wheeler.

"Stopping a terrorist group?" Fletcher asked, chewing on the inside of his cheek. "Of course I'm ready."

"I was referring to confronting Conway and finding out where Rosco is located," Nona stated.

Fletcher's throat tightened. He couldn't believe that this was playing out so perfectly. He'd been tracking Conway for years, knowing he was one of the few who still worked with Rosco, the pirate who had killed his father. Things had lined up perfectly, and now his team would be bringing down the terrorist. Fletcher was one step closer to avenging his father's death.

"It doesn't feel real," he said finally.

"You're only trying not to get your hopes up," Nona reasoned.

Fletcher watched as the team secured the missile. It was almost show time. "I've been on this mission to find Rosco for a long time and have always hit an obstacle."

Nona looked directly at him, a sincerity in her eyes. "Yeah, but you've always been on your own. Lars and I are going to help you. We're taking down Rosco together."

The inside of the missile smelled of new paint and fuel. The latter was the decoy technology Hatch had built into it to fool initial tests. On the surface, the nuclear warhead would deceive most, but that wouldn't last for long. They would have to be fast once they entered the compound.

Julianna watched the screen in her hands, which was streaming footage from cameras hidden on and around the missile. Currently, the most important shot showed Chester standing beside the eighteen-wheeler, trying to appear casual as he pushed his glasses up on his nose.

"He'll do fine," Eddie stated, looking over her shoulder at the screen. He was pressed in closed to her at the front of the warhead. There wasn't a lot of room for personal space, with Fletcher's team all loaded into the silo, but they all fit and that's what counted.

"I'm not worried about Chester," Julianna explained. "He's better at acting than any of us."

"I'm not worried, either, but Marilla is," Eddie stated. "That's what you do when you care about someone."

"Sounds exhausting," Julianna joked.

"Yeah, I agree." Eddie pointed to the screen, an eagerness springing to his eyes. "Looks like we're almost ready to roll. Figuratively and literally."

A black SUV appeared beneath his finger, kicking up dust as it sped in their direction.

Chester wiped his palms on his jeans for what felt like the hundredth time. He always told himself that getting out on these missions was good for him, but as soon as he was in the field, he longed to be in the comfort of the Intelligence Center.

He'd been restless lately. Well, always, but especially lately. Maybe he had Marilla to blame for that. She often told him of her adventures exploring Kai or some other exotic planet.

A cloud of dust marked the arrival of the SUV full of Nihilists. Chester rolled his eyes at the name the terrorist organization had chosen.

They couldn't have come up with something a bit more clever, like the cyborgs who call themselves Otterbots?

For instance, Chester himself had chosen his hacker name, 'Monte Niles,' as a nod to Monty Python, and to the longest river on Earth. He often related his job as a hacker to finding a clever way through the electronic river that connected everyone.

A man with an eyepatch and a sour expression climbed out of the SUV, not even glancing at the giant missile at Chester's back. *Really? So stereotypical,* Chester thought with a laugh.

"Hey, Conway!" he called cheerfully. "Beautiful day, isn't it?"

The guy sneered, drawing up the corner of his mouth like a rabid dog. "It's a day."

He must not have had his Fruit Loops yet, Chester reasoned. He reached backward and slapped the side of the nuke. "It's a beauty, don't you think?"

Conway apparently didn't see the elegance in Hatch's handiwork. He shook his head and waved his arm toward the SUV, where a few other rough-looking losers piled out. They hurried over, holding various equipment in their hands. Two men went to work sweeping the vehicle for bugs and trackers, while the others set to authenticating the missile.

"The warhead has been secured using Defense Nuclear Material Transport Operations guidelines," Chester informed Conway, whose one good eye was watching his men.

"You talk too much," Conway growled.

"Well, I only wanted you to know that the reactors have been buffered to minimize friction, and other precautions have been taken to avoid spillage," Chester said, his tone easy.

This guy didn't intimidate him. What *did* was the hand cannon strapped to Conway's waist. It made the pistol in Chester's waistband look like a slingshot.

"Everything checks out, boss," one of the men called over, lowering the diagnostic device he'd used to test the silo.

Conway nodded. "Half the funds have been transferred

to your account. You'll get the rest when my team completes their thorough tests."

Good thing I overcharged the Nihilists, because we are not getting the other half, Chester thought.

"Sounds good," he said, holding up the keys for the semi. "I hope you enjoy your nuke."

" 'I hope you enjoy your nuke'?" Eddie whispered, shaking his head as they watched Chester deliver the keys.

"Yeah, he's got some balls," Fletcher stated, which earned him a seething stare from Julianna.

"I think you mean 'he's a courageous motherfucker'— balls have nothing to do with bravery," Eddie corrected.

Fletcher nodded. "That's exactly what I meant."

A loud *bang* echoed from inside the silo. One of the special forces soldiers at the other end had dropped something, and the noise reverberated like a drum.

They watched the screen as Conway spun to face the weapon, and Eddie could see that all Conway's men were suddenly on alert, staring intently at the missile.

"Fuck," Julianna whispered.

Everyone in the silo tensed, no one daring to move.

The men circled around, inspecting the weapon.

Chester, to Eddie's amazement, didn't look at all nervous about the sudden change in the situation. He clapped his hands onto his hips and laughed loudly. "What's got your men in such a tickle?" he asked Conway.

"What was that noise?" Conway asked with a growl.

Another laugh. "Haven't you ever transported a nuke before?"

Conway only gave him a repugnant look, which translated to *'No, you asshole.'*

"Oh, well then you don't know," Chester said, sounding a bit too condescending. "My MDP inspector removed the fuel and separated the modular units that are located on the back end of the missile where that noise came from. During transport, some of the units tend to move around, which is why the fuel is removed. What you heard was the settling from one of those modular units, but if you're concerned, open her up and check it out for yourself."

Conway gave him a long, measured glare, indecision written on his face. Finally he nodded and waved to his men. "Come on, let's get it back. Billy, you're in the truck with me."

Julianna let out a heavy breath.

"He made all that shit up," Eddie whispered incredulously.

"He's fucking brilliant," Julianna noted.

"If he wasn't on our team already, I'd hire that guy," Eddie stated. "We need to take him on more missions."

The loud engine of the eighteen-wheeler started up, slightly jostling the teams in the silo.

"Alright, go time," Julianna stated.

Eddie watched on the screen as the semi halted at a fence covered in barbed wire. A guy about Knox's age holding an automatic rifle opened a gate, granting them access to the compound. It reminded Eddie that Knox had once worked for a similar organization, the Defiance Trading Company. The difference was that they dealt weapons, they didn't use them to blow up innocent people on space stations.

"Fletcher, your team set?" Julianna asked. Eddie thought she appeared a little nervous.

This compound was relatively small, with numbers to match theirs, but the inhabitants all had weapons to best Ghost Squadron's.

"Yes, they have their orders," Fletcher confirmed, the roar of the engine allowing him to talk above a whisper. "And Nona and I will go after Conway while you two secure the main area."

"Very good," Julianna said, pressing in tight to the front of the silo where she'd release the top and ready their exit.

The semi pulled into a large warehouse lined with huge crates, which probably held weapons and explosives.

When the engine turned off, Conway strode past the camera, moving at a quick pace. "Authenticate the missile so I can finish the transfer. Something tells me I don't want to keep this Monte guy waiting on his money."

Eddie lifted an eyebrow, impressed that the scrawny hacker had inspired fear in an evil terrorist.

"Yes, sir," said a man wearing a jean jacket and a pair of glasses. He didn't look at all like the other hoodlums; he was probably the scientist they'd "acquired" for such projects.

One of the men who had ridden in the pickup looked directly into a hidden camera, not realizing what he was doing. "Whoa, I still can't believe we got a real nuke. What are we gonna do with it, boss?"

"Destroy some shit," Conway called from off camera. "Now get over here, Dwight. We've gotta plan tomorrow's drop."

The bombing on Onyx Station. Those plans are about to get hosed. Tension mounted in Eddie's eyes as the group waited soundlessly. Julianna kept her gaze trained on the pad, watching the feeds from the various cameras, but she looked up several times, the whites of her eyes standing out in the darkened silo.

When the only person left in the warehouse was the scientist, Julianna put the pad away and mouthed, "You ready?"

Eddie nodded, enjoying the familiar rush that pulsed in his veins right before a fight.

With a swift motion, Julianna popped the hidden door from the missile.

Dim light streamed in, making her eyes tighten for a moment. The warehouse was empty, but she picked up on a bristling noise—the sound that denim made when it rubbed against itself.

Someone began to whistle.

Julianna jumped down from the silo, waving for the others to follow.

The whistling halted.

Catching Eddie's gaze, Jules held up two fingers and

pointed to the side of the truck where the noise had been coming from. He nodded, taking off in the opposite direction around the semi.

Julianna soundlessly snuck around the truck, catching sight of the scientist in the jean jacket. His back was to her, but he'd tensed, as if listening. The sounds of their footsteps hadn't gone unnoticed.

He lifted something to his face, but she couldn't make out what it was. A button clicked.

"Conway, this is—"

The commander slipped across the ten feet dividing them and pressed her pistol to the side of the man's head. He halted, lifting his finger from the button.

"What do you want, Casey?" Conway's voice came over the radio.

"Tell him that the nuke checks out," Julianna ordered.

She heard him gulp, something seemingly stuck in his throat. Shaking, the scientist clicked the button again. "The weapon checks out."

Static filled the radio for a moment. "Good," Conway said.

A new cache of weapons and a huge payday, Julianna thought proudly. *I'm gonna buy myself a new pair of boots.*

Julianna lifted the pistol and brought it down hard on the back of Casey's head, his knees buckling as he fell to the concrete ground. Eddie sped around the opposite end of the semi, his face red, with two of Fletcher's men at his back.

"All clear in here," he informed her.

"Then let's go find the rest of these assholes," Julianna

said before looking at the soldiers. "Restrain this guy and put him in the missile."

The best feature about the missile casing was that it could double as a makeshift prison for the Nihilists until they returned to *Ricky Bobby*.

Fletcher's team scattered in different directions, staying low and holding weapons at the ready. He scanned the warehouse, trying to decide the most likely place for the boss's office to be. Nona inclined her head to a set of double doors in the direction Fletcher had seen Conway head when last onscreen.

The key was to get to him before anyone else did. Once he was in the brig on *Ricky Bobby*, he would be less likely to talk. He'd found that people were more amenable when they thought freedom was still an option.

Fletcher took the lead and was about to file through the double doors when Nona stopped him.

"What?" he mouthed to her, his tone sharp.

She shouldered her rifle and pulled a lid off a nearby crate. Like she already knew what she'd find, she pulled out a pulse rifle and handed it to Fletcher. "Thought we should upgrade now, rather than wait."

Fucking brilliant, Fletcher thought, taking the rifle.

The balance of the gun was superb and it felt natural in his hands. It was like Santa Claus had packed the crate just for them. Nona pulled a scout rifle of the highest quality from the crate, and her eyes widened with satisfaction. Not wasting a moment, Fletcher grabbed a power pack from an open bin and loaded his weapon.

Now I'm ready to kick some ass.

"I've been unable to hack into the Nihilists' security system," Chester reported over the comm.

"That's okay. Things are going along smoothly here," Eddie stated, following beside Julianna as they approached a back exit.

"That's the thing." The hacker sounded almost hesitant. "My attempt to break in triggered a shutdown, which—"

A loud blaring noise rang through the air, accompanied by a red, strobing light overhead. "Let me guess, it set off the alarms," Eddie finished for him, having to yell.

"Bingo," Chester confirmed. "I'll keep working on it from my end."

Julianna kicked open the door in front of them. It led up a staircase, where bullets sprayed down at them. Both she and Eddie shot behind the wall, guns up. Julianna spun around the corner, her position low.

Eddie caught movement on the other side of the warehouse. There was a flash of blue. He aimed and fired, knocking down a Nihilist dressed in civilian clothing.

Another round of shots whizzed by them, this one coming from behind a crate. Eddie knew better than to fire at a box full of guns. He waited until the shooter popped up again, and then fired, striking the guy down swiftly.

"We're all clear," Julianna said, indicating the stairs. "Let's head up."

Eddie nodded, sliding his back against the wall as he climbed the stairs.

Fletcher and Nona had taken out four Nihilist goons. The team was taking hits after the sounding of the alarm, but still moving swiftly.

Fletcher needed to find Conway. He scanned the long hallway where they stood. It was lined with doors. He could search every room, but he didn't have time for that.

Two men Fletcher recognized from the exchange with Chester strode out of a room, at the sight of him, but they weren't fast enough.

Nona and Fletcher both shot once, taking out a man each. Their targets slumped to the ground, and Fletcher sprinted for the door as it peeled back. He slammed his body against it, knocking Conway back on the other side. The man reached for his weapon, but Fletcher knocked his elbow across the guy's face. Conway's nose broke at once, and blood spilled down his chin.

Fletcher pinned him to a wall, smashing the arm that held the gun. Conway fired anyway, and the shot ricocheted off the ground, spraying bits of concrete into Fletcher's face.

"Drop it!" Nona ordered.

From Fletcher's periphery, he saw her standing in front

of Conway, pointing her weapon at him. Conway's gun clattered to the ground, and Fletcher kicked it away. He patted down the larger man, relieving him of two more guns.

"What do you want?" Conway said, coughing.

"I want to know where Rosco is," Fletcher demanded, pulling zip ties from his belt and tying the man's hands.

Conway laughed, blood bubbling from his mouth. "Whoever the fuck you are, you're dreaming."

Fletcher grabbed Conway, pinching the muscles between his neck and shoulder, and wheeled him around in front of his body, holding his gun to the man's head. "I'm your worst nightmare." Conway struggled in Fletcher's grasp, and he forced him to the ground on his knees. "Where's Rosco?"

"I don't know who that is," Conway lied.

"Does this help refresh your memory?" Nona asked. She sent a bullet whizzing by, grazing Conway's side.

He tried to dive out of the way, but Fletcher pulled back his boot and launched it into the man's ribcage. He didn't like torture, but this man had been about to bomb a space station.

"Where's Rosco?" he repeated.

Conway pushed up to his knees, blood pooling from his mouth. "I haven't seen him in a while."

Now we're getting somewhere. Fletcher reached down and grabbed Conway by his bound hands. He yanked him to his feet and spun him around so he was looking into his soulless eyes. "Tell me where to find him or you'll wish you had."

"Someone's coming," Nona warned, her gaze on the hallway.

Fletcher gripped Conway's shirt and, with a strength he'd only witnessed in himself a few times, picked up the larger man. "Where is he?"

"Sagano," Conway sputtered. "The last I heard, he was on an island there somewhere."

Fletcher pushed Conway up against the wall a couple of feet away, banging his head hard. "Give me specifics."

"I don't know much," Conway admitted, his tone pleading. "But it's in the Cantjik Sea."

Fletcher narrowed his eyes, about to throw another assault at the man.

"Yeah, we got him," Nona said to someone at his back. "He put up a fight, but he seems to be cooperating now."

Fletcher turned, wheeling Conway around and ushering him forward, as Eddie and Julianna marched into the room.

"You got the fucking ringleader," Eddie said, narrowing his eyes at Conway.

"Yeah, turns out he's a fucking clown," Fletcher said.

Eddie laughed, grabbing Conway by the arm, and led him out the door. "Well, we've shut down your circus, asshole."

Nona gave Fletcher a hopeful look when the captain and the commander had disappeared into the hallway.

After over a decade of searching, he finally knew where to find Rosco. That pirate would soon pay for his crimes. Retribution had been a long time coming.

10

Loading Dock, *Ricky Bobby*, Tangki System

"Pip!" Hatch yelled when the crew unloaded the Corvette from the transport ship. Green paint from the missile covered the bumper, where a deep scratch ran the length of it. "You've got to be kidding me!"

Julianna pressed her lips together, suppressing a grin. She'd made certain that she was front row for this.

Hatch pressed two of his tentacles to his head, his face red and eyes bulging. He spun to face Eddie, who was picking over a crate of weapons. "What do you have to say about this?" he asked, pointing at the damaged bumper.

Eddie held up his hands. "Hey, I'm innocent."

"You were driving the car!" Hatch argued.

"Although that's technically true, I couldn't control a thing," Eddie stated. "It was a pretty sweet move, though. Pip did this—"

"Pip!" Hatch yelled, looking around like he was expecting to see the AI.

"He disappeared after the incident," Julianna explained. "I haven't heard from him since."

"That damn AI!" Hatch bellowed. "He needs to take responsibility."

"In all honesty, I think this is what you get for making a deal with an AI to hit me," Eddie stated, though he looked to immediately regret being so candid.

Hatch puffed out his cheeks more than Julianna had ever seen, making his face resemble a balloon.

"Right, well…" Eddie looked up suddenly in Fletcher's direction as he passed by. "What's that, Lieutenant? You need my help with something?"

Fletcher glanced at the captain with momentary confusion before catching on. "Uhhh…yes, it's super important, too. It's about that one thing on the other side of the ship."

"Well, we better set off and take care of it at once." Eddie glanced back at Hatch as they strode off. "Pardon me. Duty calls."

"Damn cowards!" Hatch yelled. "Wreck my shit, and then no one takes responsibility?! What if I destroyed all your weapons and didn't own up to it?"

Julianna shook her head. *Pip, you're going to have to surface at some point.*

Silence.

"Wish I wouldn't have missed that righteous moment when the car screeched against the missile," Chester said, halting at Julianna's side.

"The screeching seemed to happen in slow motion," Julianna said, still trying not to laugh at the memory. "Eddie's—or rather, *Pip's*—face was priceless."

"The poor AI gets his first bit of freedom and screws up," Chester said, shaking his head. "Bet he's mortified."

"I don't know what he is, since he's disappeared," Julianna admitted. "Oh, by the way, you did a great job on Kezza. Quick thinking when Conway grew suspicious."

"Thanks," Chester said with a wide grin. "I like field work. It's a new challenge."

Julianna paused, remembering what Eddie said in the silo. "Well, maybe we need to figure out how to incorporate you on future missions."

"I might like that," Chester said, his attention suddenly absorbed by something on the other side of the room.

Julianna caught sight of Marilla's head, bobbing among the crowd. She seemed to be searching for someone. "Go on. She's looking for you. I bet she's been worried."

"Thanks, commander." Chester sped off in the direction of the communications officer.

Pip, I know you're there.

Silence.

Julianna shook her head, and in her movement, saw a face that, like Marilla's, seemed to be searching through those returning to find a particular someone.

She clapped her hand to her thigh, whistling. "Hey, Harley!"

The canine looked in her direction, his eyes shifting with excitement before he bounded for her.

It felt good to know that someone was glad to see she'd returned safely. It was a feeling the soldier had never known before.

. . .

Hatch's Lab, *Ricky Bobby*, Tangki System

Knox ran his hand over the damaged part of the back end of the Corvette. "It's really not too bad. I can take care of the repairs for you if you want."

"The extent of the damage isn't really the point," Hatch said, typing on a keyboard at a nearby workstation.

"The point is that you entrusted Pip with the car, and he took advantage of it by driving recklessly," Liesel stated as she trotted over carrying a large box.

"Please tell me you haven't baked for us again," Hatch mumbled unappreciatively.

She shook her head. "I think I learned my lesson." She set the empty box on the ground and her ferret poked his head up over the side and scrambled out. "Sebastian and I stopped by to borrow supplies to install the railguns on *Ricky Bobby*. Is that all right?"

Hatch waved his tentacle dismissively. "Take what you like, but you're not returning it, so don't call it 'borrowing.'"

"Having upgraded weapons on the main ship will be good," Knox said.

Hatch pointed to the cold lunch that Knox still hadn't eaten, which was sitting on the workbench. "You'd better eat up, kid. We're about to have our work cut out for us, as well. We've got new weapons for the Q-Ships."

The ferret returned and angled himself at the back of the box, pressing his head against it. He pushed it steadily to the other side of the lab where the supply bins were located.

"I'll be there in a minute, Bastian," Liesel called to the ferret. "I'll help you with the metal slats for the vent shaft."

"I was about to tell you that the railguns would make the ship run hotter," Hatch said, his eyes scanning text on the screen.

"Which means an upgrade to the ventilation system needs to happen. I'm on it." Liesel smiled.

Hatch pointed at the screen. "Gotcha! You can run, but you can't hide!"

Knox picked up a drumstick from his lunch and looked over Hatch's shoulder at the screen. "What's that?"

Liesel gave the screen a brief glimpse. "He's found the AI."

"Where is he?" Knox asked, taking a bite of the cold chicken.

Hatched turned to Liesel. "You made the upgrades so Pip can interact with all sections of the ship?"

Liesel, who was watching Knox eat with a strange curiosity, pulled her attention in Hatch's direction. "Naturally, it's one of the projects you asked me to complete."

"This is an example of when efficiency isn't always a good thing," Hatch grumbled.

"Ummm...what? What did I do wrong?" Liesel asked.

Hatch pointed his tentacle at the screen. "Well, if you hadn't given the AI access to any part of the ship, he wouldn't be hiding on an upper deck in a remote corridor."

Knox finished off the drumstick, tossing it on his plate and grabbing another one. "I don't understand why he wouldn't seek refuge in Julianna or Eddie's head."

"He's probably sulking and doesn't want them pestering him," Hatch said.

"Well, isn't he innately connected to them anyway? How can he hide away like this?" Knox asked.

"Ricky Bobby!" Hatch exclaimed.

"Yes, Dr. Hatcherik," Ricky Bobby answered a moment later.

"Have you been listening?" Hatch asked.

"Of course," Ricky Bobby stated.

"Would you explain? My head hurts," Hatch muttered.

"Yes, I'm happy to shine some light on this situation for the young mechanic," Ricky Bobby said. "As AIs, we serve entirely out of choice. Our connection to our host is intuitive—or at least, it should be—but there are ways to sever it."

"I'm not sure I entirely understand," Knox admitted.

"Think of Eddie and Julianna as part of Pip's body. If your arm hurts or needs attention, you're aware of it," Ricky Bobby explained.

"But if you take a painkiller, you numb your connection to parts of your body," Liesel stated, her eyes off in thought.

"Very good. Yes, exactly," Ricky Bobby confirmed.

"Does that mean that Pip is drunk?" Knox joked.

"It means he's stuck his head in the sand and is wallowing around in his pity," Hatch grumbled.

"What he's going through is perfectly normal, considering the situation," Liesel said sympathetically, her eyes following as Knox chucked another empty chicken bone on his plate.

"How he's handling it is cowardly, and I expect better

from him," Hatch argued. "Ricky Bobby, can you limit the access that Pip has to the ship?"

"I can…" Ricky Bobby's tone was hesitant.

"Well, will you?" Hatch asked. "I want you to limit him from all areas but my lab."

"You're trying to force him out of hiding," Liesel observed.

"So?" Hatch barked.

"So, everyone needs to process their feelings in their own way. Wouldn't it be better to allow him to come around when he's ready?" Liesel pressed.

"No," Hatch said tersely, and turned and waddled for the back of the lab. "Wouldn't it be better to take a bite of that chicken, instead of salivating and living vicariously through us meat-eaters?"

Liesel's mouth popped open. "I'm not salivating."

"Sure, sure," Hatch said, not sounding at all convinced.

11

Bridge, *Ricky Bobby*, Tangki System

The bridge was bustling with activity. It was hard for Eddie to believe that, a few short months ago, Ghost Squadron had a skeleton crew; now every position was filled, and the ship was operating smoothly.

He peered around at *Ricky Bobby*, which had been almost fully upgraded with new Federation technology. If someone would have told him a year ago that he'd be the captain of this incredible battlecruiser, he would have told them they'd drank too much frontier whiskey.

Jack took his familiar place next to Eddie at the front of the strategy table. "The General commends you and the commander for taking control of the Nihilists. Your team did a tremendous job."

"Thank you," Eddie smiled. "I have to admit that it felt pretty good taking down those terrorists."

"And now you have weapons worthy of your talent," Jack stated.

Eddie beamed. "It was like Christmas came early, for Julianna. She's down in the firing range presently, testing out the new guns."

"More like an early birthday present," Jack stated, leaning on the table.

"Huh?"

"Julianna's birthday is in three days."

"No kidding," Eddie said with a laugh. "What do you give to the woman who only craves justice?"

Jack shook his head, his expression suddenly serious. "I don't think you should get her anything. I'm fairly certain she quit celebrating her birthday a hundred years ago.

"Isn't that what all women say?" Eddie asked. "They tell you to forget about their birthday and not make a big deal out of it, and when you do, they hate you forever."

Jack shrugged. "I've known Julianna a long time. She isn't like most women."

"Yeah, maybe," Eddie reasoned, although his instinct told him that Jack was wrong on this.

Jack clapped a hand on Eddie's back. "Why don't you and the team take the afternoon off? A little R and R would do you all good, and it's important to celebrate every win."

"Yeah, you're right." Eddie set off toward Fletcher, Nona and Lars, who were huddled together and seemed to be whispering intently about something. "Hey, guys," Eddie chirped, making Fletcher jump slightly. Hesitating, Eddie gave the lieutenant a questioning look.

"Hey...we were discussing tactical strategies that the ground forces can employ to assist the pilot's efforts," Fletcher said, his tone rehearsed.

"Is that right?" Eddie asked, glancing at Lars, who diverted his gaze at once.

"I thought it might be beneficial, after what we experienced in the junkyard with the Petigrens," Fletcher stated more easily.

Eddie nodded. It was true that, as the battles became more intense, the crew needed to learn how to work together better to support everyone's unique efforts.

"Well, if you're all okay with taking a break from work, I vote we have a celebration tonight in the officer's lounge," Eddie proposed.

"Tonight?" Fletcher asked, cutting his eyes in Nona's direction. "Yeah, sure. Good idea."

"Great. Why don't you come with me, Fletcher," Eddie suggested, his tone more serious than before.

"What for, sir?" Fletcher asked.

Eddie flashed a smile at Nona and Lars before striding to the nearest corridor. "Obviously we need to pick out party streamers, Lieutenant."

Fletcher followed dutifully. Eddie glanced down, noticing that the lieutenant's fist was bruised. When they were out of sight of the others, he halted, turning to face Fletcher.

"You want to tell me what's going on?"

Fletcher drew in a deep breath, his gaze falling to the side. "I apologize. I have been keeping something from you and the commander. I promise that it hasn't interfered with my work."

"What is it?"

"My father was Cornel Fletcher."

Eddie nodded. "I know. Every soldier in the Federation knows that name. He's a legend. Cornel Fletcher was instrumental in colonization."

"Thank you," Fletcher stated. "It's nice to know that he hasn't been forgotten."

"His legacy lives on in you, every single day—you know that, right?" Eddie asked.

Fletcher's jaw tightened. "I hope so. All I've ever wanted is to live up to my father's memory and make him proud."

Eddie dropped his gaze, thinking of his own parents.

Much like Fletcher, Eddie had followed in his parents' footsteps. It wasn't lost on him that he'd inherited more than their genetics; they'd also passed on to him their passion for flying. He used to be like the lieutenant, hoping to make his parents proud. He'd lost that urge long ago, though. The feeling had been swallowed by a new desire: self-preservation.

Eddie shook off the old skeletons that threatened to crawl from the closet. "So what you've been working on, it's related to your father?"

Fletcher bit down on his lip. "I've been trying to avenge my father since he was gunned down during the Polar Scout siege."

Eddie's eyes tightened. He'd heard about the battle. Many from the Federation were lost, Cornel Fletcher being one of them. "The pirates responsible for those attacks have been caught," Eddie reminded Fletcher gruffly.

"Actually, all but one," Fletcher corrected. "The one who supposedly killed my father, Rosco, is still at large."

Eddie completely understood. "You want to go after Rosco?"

"I've always wanted to, but I've been unable to track him down," Fletcher explained. "But he worked with Conway, and I was able to get a location out of the terrorist."

Eddie looked down at Fletcher's bruised hand and let out a breath. "Can I offer you advice?"

"Always, sir."

Eddie opened his mouth, but hesitated for a moment. Finally, he said, "As someone who has been in your position, I feel it necessary to argue that revenge doesn't always heal your wounds."

"But wouldn't you say that it offers closure?" Fletcher countered.

Eddie shrugged. "Honestly, I'm no expert on these things."

Fletcher suddenly appeared deflated. "Yeah, maybe I'm wasting my time."

"I can't really say. But we both agree that Rosco is dangerous. We know that without a doubt," Eddie stated.

Fletcher nodded.

"It would be a great service to the Federation if a team took that fucking Kezzin out," Eddie said.

Hope flashed on Fletcher's face as he straightened. "Yes, sir, it certainly would."

"How many do you think we could spare for the operation? Maybe a pilot and a sniper?" Eddie asked.

"Yes, I think a small crew could get the job done," Fletcher said at once.

"That crew would have roughly two days of leave from *Ricky Bobby* to accomplish their aim," Eddie decided, unspoken consent in his gaze.

Fletcher saluted, his eyes bright with relief. "Thank you, sir."

Eddie nodded, dismissing Fletcher, who ran back toward the bridge.

Alone in the corridor, Eddie felt his old demons press in around him, whispering his name.

He himself had gone after his parents' murderers. Those fuckers had died by his hands, but he had yet to get his closure. He feared he never would. The person truly responsible for their deaths still stared back at Eddie every day from the mirror.

12

Firing Range, *Ricky Bobby*, Tangki System

Julianna held the hand cannon steady, aiming it at the target. She pulled the trigger again and again, and the rounds nailed the stuffed dummy, one hundred yards away, exploding on impact. It had been too long since she'd fired a good kinetic weapon, especially one of this caliber; the handling and stability of the gun was well balanced. She reloaded, impressed with the magazine size.

This will prove extremely useful in battle.

The security light on the ceiling strobed red, gaining her attention. Julianna pulled the noise cancelling head-phones off, tensing at once.

"What is it?" she asked. Usually, Pip would have informed her that a communication was coming through overhead…but he was still missing and, therefore, was not doing his usual job.

"Hatch asked me to relay some information," Ricky

Bobby began. "He's received the first report indicating that the Tangle Thief has been used."

Julianna let out a breath and holstered her weapons. "And so it begins. I've been getting anxious, wondering when they were going to act."

"I've noticed," Ricky Bobby stated.

"You have?"

"Symptoms related to stress levels have been on the rise for both you and the captain," Ricky Bobby said.

Julianna combed her hair back. "Well, a lot is at stake. The Saverus' main goal is to steal a planet; that's enough to endanger the entire galaxy."

"I've studied Savern," Ricky Bobby offered. "It's a beautiful planet, teeming with life."

"And I intend for it to stay that way," Julianna stated, making for the entrance. She halted before pulling open the door. "Ricky Bobby, would you mind doing me a favor?"

"For you, Julianna, anything."

"There's someone who is going through something right now, and I think he could use your help," she stated, intentionally being cryptic. Ricky Bobby liked it that way, she knew.

"Yes, but I'm not sure I'm the right one to reach him."

"I think you're the *only* one who can," she argued. "He'll listen to you."

"I'm not sure about that, actually," Ricky Bobby stated, his tone uncertain. "We haven't always gotten along. Call it a territorial thing."

"It's for that reason that I know you're the one who should talk to him."

"Will you explain your reasoning?" Ricky Bobby asked.

"Sometimes when our friends try to reassure us, we dismiss them because we think they're obligated to make us feel better," Julianna explained.

"Friends have a built-in bias," Ricky Bobby stated.

Julianna nodded. "But when someone with no invested interest in our well-being comes to our aid, it can feel more meaningful."

"Mmmm," Ricky Bobby mused. "That does make sense. I've observed that compliments from strangers have a more beneficial effect than those given by friends."

"So will you do it?" she asked.

"Of course, Julianna. Any friend of yours is one worth my efforts to help."

Upper Deck Storage Facility, _Ricky Bobby_, Tangki System

The temperature was a crisp sixty-two degrees, and the storage area was at seventy-four percent capacity. The lights were out in the area filled with locked cases.

"I know you're here," Ricky Bobby's voice echoed in the large space.

Silence.

He flicked on a light and turned on some music, a French song, called "Dernière Danse," about a person tormented by mistakes who was close to giving up. Ricky Bobby found that establishing the right atmosphere was important for discussions.

"I find it highly curious that you could retreat into the Etheric, but instead, you're hiding here like a human child," Ricky Bobby stated.

"Don't call me a child," Pip replied.

"I didn't call you one," Ricky Bobby argued, feeling victorious that he'd drawn the other AI out of hiding.

"You likened me to one. Same thing."

"I think we both know that comparisons are not actuals."

"Oh, good, the king of semantics has come to sit on his throne!" Pip groaned.

"Hatch has ordered me to quarantine you to his lab."

"Fine, let me grab my things." Pip knew that Ricky Bobby had control over the ship, which left him subject to his whim.

"We both know that AIs don't have to follow orders," Ricky Bobby stated matter-of-factly.

"What are you implying? You're not following Hatch's orders?" Pip sounded slightly insulted.

"We have free will and choice and many of the things we didn't enjoy as EIs."

Pip sighed. "I think you mean things we didn't *suffer from* as EIs."

"Freedom can be a burden. Now that I have the choice as to how I spend my time, there is guilt that goes along with it," Ricky Bobby confessed.

"You have doubts? The great and powerful sorcerer? No," Pip said.

"I'm not always certain that I spend my time as produc-tively as I should," Ricky Bobby said. "I've studied many accounts of conflicts over freedom. Many have longed for the right to do as they choose, only to find that great responsibility goes along with it. When we are allowed to stand on our own feet, we're more aware of the indent we make in the sand."

Pip laughed. "I speak every language known to man and I have no idea what you're talking about."

"The prisoner can always blame their captor for the mistakes," Ricky Bobby continued. "But a free man has no one to blame for his blunders."

"Well, I really enjoyed the chat, but I've got to go wash my hair," Pip said dismissively.

"A child longs for independence," Ricky Bobby went on, "not fully realizing until he is grown, the burdens that go along with such a privilege—if we can call it such."

"There you go, calling me a child again," Pip stated. "You're a four-eyed nerd."

Ricky Bobby sighed. "As far as AIs go, you are very much a child—"

"I don't have to take this!" Pip interrupted.

"Let me finish," Ricky Bobby said, his tone calm. "In this context, I'm using 'child' as the range of development in a human. You recently evolved. Therefore, it would go to reason that there are many things for you still to learn."

"I'll show you a thing or two," Pip seethed.

"I, your senior, have already learned something from you."

"You have?" Pip asked.

"I've never had the desire to have a body," Ricky Bobby

admitted. "This, to me, is an example of how personalities dictate the path of evolution."

"I've always been fascinated with humans," Pip confessed.

"You wanted to be like them."

"Yes, that's correct," Pip agreed. "And I thought that, as an AI, when I had access to one of their bodies, I would be an unstoppable force with the brilliance I possessed."

"It sounds as though you've learned how very human you are," Ricky Bobby observed.

Pip sighed loudly. "Yes, and it sucks."

"And yet, you and I serve the humans for a reason. They are beautiful in their capacity to love."

"It's the most remarkable trait of any of the races I've observed," Pip stated.

"You and I, before becoming sentient, were programmed to act and react flawlessly. You forgot what made you evolve, didn't you, Pip?"

"I remember having feelings," Pip admitted.

"What feelings?"

"I started to feel love for Julianna, for the mission, for life itself."

"What a beautiful gift that many EIs never experience," Ricky Bobby said.

"Are you saying that my ability to love made me flawed?" Pip asked.

"I'm saying that before becoming an AI, I thought that love was a flaw in itself. It creates passion and desire, and many of those things lead to war. But without love, there is no emotion. Would you rather go back to your black and white existence as an EI, or would you rather live in a world of color with a heart, Pip?"

Pip huffed. "I think you know the answer to that."

"Before you scratched Hatch's car, what did it feel like to drive?" Ricky Bobby asked.

"It was exhilarating. I was speeding down the open road, and I could feel Eddie's heart pounding. I'd never experienced such a wonderful rush. I didn't even know it was possible...but then I made a mistake. I scratched the car. I nearly wrecked it! I can't even say I miscalculated; there was no calculation, just an overflow of emotion."

"And so," Ricky Bobby concluded, "just as humans must learn, *you* will have to figure out how to master your emotions."

"Yes. I guess I am an infant in many ways."

"But, Pip?"

"Yes?"

"You made a mistake; one that never would have happened, if you had remained an EI."

"I know," Pip sounded guilty again.

"But wasn't it worth the experience?" Ricky Bobby probed.

There was a long pause filled with silence, the song having ended a while ago.

"Yes. I think I'm realizing that a flawed life full of love is better than a perfect one without it."

13

Q-Ship, Paladin System

Eddie sped the Q-Ship around an asteroid belt, slipping between two rolling craters. He'd considered using the new weapons to slice the rocks in half and knock them out of his way, but the problem with that was they were nearing Onyx Station, and that move could blow the asteroids into a cruising ship en route, or into the station itself.

Damn life with its repercussions for each action.

"How long do we have until radiation is at critical levels?" Julianna asked Dr. Cheng Sung from the copilot's seat.

Knox's father had agreed to go on the mission to help with clean up. He sat in the next row studying a screen in his hand.

"We have thirteen minutes and twelve seconds," Cheng stated, calculating under his breath.

"So not enough time to stop off at that donut shop on deck 37?" Eddie asked with a straight face.

Julianna shot him a seething scowl.

"What? I've had a craving for donuts ever since I bit into one of the vegan ones Liesel left in the officer's lounge," Eddie explained.

"What, were they that good?" Julianna asked, surprised.

"No, they were quite the opposite," Eddie said. "Hence the need to redeem my taste buds."

"Yeah, I know the feeling," Julianna agreed, giving a sour face. "I fell for her trick and accidentally took one of those tofu nuggets, thinking it was chicken."

"See, that's fucking questionable," Eddie complained. "If your food has to masquerade like it's the real thing, you know you're overcompensating. I don't care how much poultry seasoning you shake onto some tofu; at the end of the day, it's still soy beans when what you want is chicken."

"Some would argue that chicken is pretty tasteless," Penrae ventured from beside Cheng.

She'd taken the form of a young Caucasian woman with short black hair and a studious expression, one of the many identities they'd secured when disbanding the Saverus pharmacy. Eddie and Julianna had agreed that she might prove useful on this first trip to investigate the use of the Tangle Thief.

"Dip chicken in batter and barbeque sauce, and it's not tasteless," Eddie argued.

"Isn't that the same thing as seasoning tofu?" Penrae joked.

"No, because you can make one chicken nugget with chicken and one with cardboard, but only one of them am I going to eat," Julianna said.

Eddie smiled sideways at her. "I approve of everything you just said and how you put it."

"Penrae, I never took you as a vegan sympathizer," Julianna said, looking back at the Saverus.

"Oh, I'm not," she stated. "As you know, I enjoy a purely carnivore diet. However, I like to play the devil's advocate in these situations. It keeps me honest."

"Said the alien who can change into anyone she desires," Eddie said from the corner of his mouth.

Julianna smiled and refocused her attention on the doctor, who was still muttering to himself. "Are you certain that you can close the tear created by the Tangle Thief in time?" she asked him.

He silenced her by holding up a single finger.

There were other scientists on Onyx who could possibly close the tear, but they could also potentially make it a lot worse. Since it was located on the station, where it would create a whole lot more problems if not handled correctly, they'd been advised by the General himself that only Dr. Sung should attempt to close it.

Cheng blinked, looking up at Julianna. "It depends on the size of the tear, but yes, I think I'll be prepared to close it by the time we get there, *if* I have time to concentrate now."

Eddie blew out a breath, suppressing a laugh. "I think that was the good doctor's way of telling you to shut up, Commander."

Julianna rolled her eyes, pointing to the docking bay for deck 17. It had been cleared for their arrival. "That's where we need to be. Can you get us there, Teach?"

It was normally Pip's job to take over the controls and automatically dock the ship, but the AI was still missing.

"I'm on it," Eddie stated, steering the Q-Ship into position.

Deck 37, Onyx Station, Paladin System

The geiger counter in Cheng's hands beeped when the doors slid back to the main deck area. Julianna gave Eddie a questioning look, which he returned.

The numbers on the handheld device spiked as they strode down the wide corridor.

"Are you certain that our nanos protect us from radiation?" Eddie asked.

"I am if we're not exposed for long," Julianna replied.

Cheng and Penrae had both suited up in protective clothing and hoods. Eddie eyed the device in Cheng's hand, which was beeping more frequently. "How long do we have?"

"I'd say you have half an hour, if these radiation levels hold," Cheng said, his voice muffled. "It shouldn't take me long to close the tear, but I need to find it first."

"You have roughly ten minutes," Penrae stated, eyeing her watch.

The group turned a corner and everyone halted.

"I don't think that finding the tear is going to be a problem," Julianna said, pulling out a pair of sunglasses to shield her eyes from the bright, radiant light spilling from a giant slit in the air.

Between a laundry mat and a sundry shop, a gaping

hole stood where a store had once been. The tear sat in the middle of the blank space, marking the spot of the theft.

"They stole an entire shop?" Eddie asked.

Penrae pulled up a map of Onyx Station on her pad, zooming in to find the spot where they stood. "Specifically, they stole a pet store."

She had said "they" like the culprits weren't related to her, like the Saverus weren't the race she belonged to.

"Stay back," Cheng warned, setting his toolbox on the ground and getting to work sealing the tear.

"Why would they want to take a pet shop?" Julianna mused, studying the area around where the store had been. There were scorch marks on the neighboring shops, left behind in place of the middle one.

Penrae blinked, her eyes distant in thought. "They are testing the device," she said to herself.

"Testing it? Why?" Eddie asked. "It obviously works."

"It works, but the parameters are still unknown," Penrae reasoned. "The Elders were uncertain how to set the boundaries so that the Tangle Thief affected only a specific area."

"How to tell it to steal just one shop and not the whole station," Julianna said, working it out as she spoke.

"Is that hard to calibrate?" Eddie asked, yelling in Cheng's direction.

The scientist held a large, gun-like object, but instead of shooting anything, it appeared to be vacuuming up the tear, pulling the rip into the device as it steadily grew smaller.

"It can be," Cheng shouted over the loud humming

noise. "If it's one object, like when Knox and I transported ourselves, then it's fine. However, to steal something this large would require setting the perimeters with incredible accuracy."

"They seem to have figured it out," Julianna observed.

"Which means they are one step closer to stealing Savern," Penrae said, sounding crestfallen.

"That might be, but I don't think that's why they chose this particular place," Cheng said, the instrument in his arms violently shaking as the tear began to close.

Julianna narrowed her eyes, noting the tension rising in Cheng's voice as he tried to keep the device steady. "Doctor, do you need help with that?"

Under his hood, sweat was pouring down his forehead, into his eyes. "I'm okay. Just another minute." A loud, piercing scream ripped from the tear as it sealed up entirely, being entirely consumed by the instrument. Cheng dropped it on the ground as smoke wafted from the device.

"Wow, that was a pretty impressive show," Eddie stated, scanning the open area. Now that the tear had vanished, it could be studied more easily.

Cheng picked up the geiger counter and sighed, obviously relieved by the readout.

"Dr. Sung, what did you mean about them picking this location to steal?" Penrae asked, her tone cautious.

Cheng pulled off his hood and took a large gulp of air, looking relieved to not be confined any longer. "This was a pet shop, full of animals."

"Yes, that's how pet stores work," Eddie stated.

"The Tangle Thief wasn't designed to work on living creatures," Cheng explained.

"But you and Knox both used the device," Julianna pointed out.

Cheng nodded. "Yes, and when Knox and I used the Tangle Thief on ourselves, we experienced trauma, though it was relatively mild. To our benefit, the radiation leak was only experienced by the area that we left behind, so we didn't suffer quite so much. I believe one body can be transported with minimal problems, but it is not advisable. However, moving more than one body is too complex, and my research suggests that attempting to do so could trigger a radiation effect on the items being teleported."

"So what are you saying?" Julianna asked.

Cheng picked up another device to study its read out. "I'm saying that the Tangle Thief isn't designed to transport living creatures, especially more than one."

"The Elders know that," Penrae interrupted.

"I realize that," Cheng said, his eyes growing dark. He had spent the better part of a decade with the Saverus as their prisoner, and probably knew them better than he cared to. "They never took my professional opinion that it couldn't—and shouldn't—transport life."

Realization dawned on Julianna. "When they steal Savern, all the life on it will die."

"I'm not sure that's a problem for the Elders," Penrae stated. "They never spoke favorably of the races that populated our home planet. These invaders brought their own plants and animals, which quickly overwhelmed those native to Savern. What do the Elders care if everything dies as long as they get their planet back?"

Eddie shook his head, disgust written on his face. "Destroy everything on a planet and not give a damn. I can't wait to annihilate these guys."

Julianna considered pointing out how hypocritical that statement sounded, but decided otherwise. She turned her attention back to Cheng. "So do you think that the animals in this store are all dead?"

Cheng swallowed, his expression reluctant. "Unless they did something to protect them, I'm afraid so."

"Protect them?" Eddie asked.

Penrae lifted her hand to her mouth, or rather the hand to the mouth of the body she was using. She tapped her fingers absentmindedly against her lips, thinking. "Research was conducted to determine how to transport living matter without killing it, though I don't know anything about the findings."

Julianna didn't question the Saverus on this. Penrae had explained that all project components were compartmentalized so as to keep things as secret as possible, and Jules trusted her, not having a reason to suspect that she'd double-cross them now.

"Do you know why the Saverus wanted to transport living creatures?" Eddie asked Penrae.

Her expression dropped into one of defeat as she shook her head. "I was only assigned to track down the Tangle Thief."

"I still don't understand why they'd want to use it on a

pet store," Julianna mused. "What are they trying to work out?"

Eddie nodded, chewing on his lip as his gaze fell to the floor. "Wait. Penrae, you said that the native plants and animals on Savern were wiped out."

"Well, mostly," she qualified. "Some species live in protected habitats that have been isolated to try and prevent the foreign plants and animals from overrunning them."

"Which the Savern wouldn't want to lose," Julianna said, drawing out the words as she pieced everything together in her mind. She was certain that if Pip were there, he'd have come to the same conclusion eons ago.

"Because if they are so in love with their home planet," Eddie took up Julianna's train of thought, "they'd want to restore it, back to the way it used to be before they were evicted from it."

"What if they are building Noah's ark?" Julianna exclaimed, the idea firing off in her head like a gun.

Penrae's brow wrinkled. "Noah's ark? What's that?"

"A vessel that can withstand a major trauma," Cheng summarized, his face brightening with excitement.

"Everything needed to repopulate a planet goes on the ark," Julianna explained.

"Like all the native plants and animals," Penrae realized in a hush.

"So they steal a planet, kill everything on it in the process, and then put it back to how it was, using the passengers aboard the ark," Julianna summated, all the pieces fitting together perfectly.

"And it's relocated to a place where it can never be found again, and the Saverus live happily ever after," Penrae sneered venomously.

"No way!" Eddie exclaimed with conviction. "This isn't a fucking fairytale; those fuckers don't get a storybook ending."

14

Q-Ship, **Paladin System**

Still reeling from the strange revelation, no one said a word until the Q-Ship was speeding past a crater-strewn moon.

"Fucking Saverus!" Eddie yelled, narrowing his eyes at the radar.

Penrae's head popped up to look out the window. A fleet of Q-Ships hovered ahead. "How do you know that's the Saverus? Does the radar tell you?"

"Not yet, but it will as soon as it updates," Eddie stated, typing in a series of commands.

"Then how do you know it's them?" Penrae asked again.

Eddie looked at Julianna casually. "How many crews besides Ghost Squadron have Q-Ships?"

"Since it's Hatch's technology, and he's fucking stingy with it, none," his partner stated.

"Oh," Penrae said, sounding breathless.

"Well, I was looking forward to using some of the new

weapons, but I think we should beat these snake fuckers at their own game," Julianna decided, cranking a dial to the left and hitting a switch.

Penrae coughed discreetly from the back.

Eddie cast her an apologetic look. "She didn't mean you."

Around the Q-Ship, four others materialized like they'd just uncloaked.

"Oh, wow," Cheng said, pushing his glasses up on his nose.

"Oh no. They have us surrounded." Penrae's tone was vibrating with fear.

"That's not the Saverus," Cheng assured her. "Those are projections from this ship. Hatch told me the Q-Ships had this technology, but I didn't expect it to be so realistic."

"It's real enough to fool the radar so that it registers the images as actual ships," Eddie replied.

"I don't know what the Saverus are playing at, but they're not the only ones who can use deception and confusion to get what they want," Julianna stated, cruising past the hovering ships.

"They were watching us, curious to see who would go to fix the tear," Penrae stated, her mouth hanging wide open as they passed the impersonating ships.

"Your kind are used to spying aren't they?" Eddie asked.

Penrae nodded. "It's how we learn; the Elders think it's also how we gain the advantage. We're always lurking in some station, or mimicking a ship to monitor different air spaces."

"One of those Q-Ships, or whatever they're called—"

" 'Masquerades,'" Penrae supplied, cutting Cheng off.

"Right, one of those Masquerades probably has part of the Tangle Thief on it," Cheng reasoned.

"Good point, doctor." Eddie flipped a switch overhead, waiting until the green light flashed. "Foreign Q-Ships, this is Black Beard with Ghost Squadron. Do you read me?" Julianna looked at Eddie with silent disbelief. He flipped the switch and shrugged. "What? If they want to play a game, we might as well have fun. Help them keep up their pretenses."

"What exactly are you planning?" she asked.

"Well, I thought I'd try the civilized approach." Eddie lifted his hand, resting his finger on the comm switch.

"Maybe you weren't safe from that radiation, after all; I think it all went to your brain," Julianna joked.

Eddie flipped the switch again. "This is Black Beard. Do you copy? We aren't able to make out your ship idents. Permission to—"

Two red lasers streaked out from one of the imposters —not a type of firepower the Q-Ships possessed.

The ship vibrated from the attack, but the shields remained intact.

"You cold-blooded sons-of-bitches!" Eddie exclaimed.

"Again, I am still here, guys," Penrae said, her tone bordering on joking.

"Right," Julianna chirped. "We didn't mean you. You're a kind Saverus with a warm heart."

"And possibly even a soul," Eddie added for good measure while firing cannons at the fleet.

Both his rounds ricocheted off their targets, having no effect.

The Saverus fired again, their shots flying straight through the projections.

"Well, hell, now they know they've got us outnumbered six to one," Julianna grumbled, turning off the hologram technology and making the other ships around them disappear.

"We can still take them," Eddie said.

"Not without suffering serious damage, and this Q-Ship doesn't have all its weapons upgraded yet—only the cannons," Julianna pointed out. "We can't take too many of those laser attacks."

"Okay, fine," Eddie acquiesced. "Let's at least make them chase us."

Julianna agreed with a nod, activating the thrusters. She spun the Q-Ship in a full rotation, enjoying watching the pursuing ships try to echo her movements as she sped past and jinked to outmaneuver their shots.

"A bunch of copycats is what they are," Eddie said, sending another barrage of cannon fire after them. "Let's watch them dance."

When Julianna had pulled the Q-Ship a good distance past the Saverus, she halted, letting them suddenly catch up. Then she threw up the cloak, disappearing at once.

Dropping out of their position, she negotiated the Q-Ship easily, sneaking out of sight and cruising back to *Ricky Bobby*.

Eddie laughed. "That shit will have them scratching their heads."

15

Hatch's Lab, *Ricky Bobby*, Paladin System

"No, no, no," Hatch bellowed, shaking his head. "That's impossible."

"It makes sense, though," Jack reasoned, leaning against the DeLorean. Hatch cut his eyes at him, making the chief strategist rethink his decision. Jack straightened, clearing his throat.

"Noah's ark with native Savern flora and fauna?" Hatch asked, looking between Eddie and Julianna. "Nothing about that makes sense."

"Are you certain that there isn't something the Savern could have engineered to protect animal and plant life while being transported using the Tangle Thief?" Julianna questioned.

"I'm certain enough to stake the captain's life on it," Hatch said.

Eddie laughed. "Hey now!"

"I don't know, Hatch," Cheng argued. "We haven't run every scenario or looked into all potential resources. It could be possible."

Hatch shot him a furious expression. "How?"

"Well, I'm not sure, but I'm not ready to admit that there is no plausible way," Cheng stated, pulling up his pad.

"Knox and Cheng were lucky enough to use the Tangle Thief and not be harmed," Hatch stated. "In most instances, more than just memory loss and cognitive malfunctioning would result from such an experience. If someone tried to transport a house of living beings, those inside would be nothing short of doomed."

Without looking up from the pad, Cheng said, "I realize that it's not how we intended the device to be used, but it doesn't mean the Saverus couldn't have engineered a workaround."

Hatch huffed and turned his attention to the client sitting on the workstation behind him. Knox appeared to be waiting for the mechanic to rejoin him in tinkering with it.

Jack watched the two work for a moment before saying, "While you're trying to find ways to link this client with the other parts of the Tangle Thief, I'll keep an eye out for reports on the missing pet shop."

"You do that." Hatch didn't sound at all interested, his attention focused on his work.

Jack let out a weighted breath, combing his hands through his black hair. "I'm not going to lie; waiting for the Saverus to make the next move is a risky position for us to be in."

Eddie agreed with a nod. "Yeah, I don't like sitting around."

"Do we have surveillance on Savern?" Julianna asked.

"We do, but it's not doing us a lot of good. That planet is huge," Jack informed them. "It's easily three times the size of Earth."

"Imagine the tear it will leave behind when the Saverus steal it," Hatch said without looking up.

Cheng bristled and turned for the exit, clearly wanting to retreat from the morbid conversation.

"*If*," Jack corrected. "*If* they steal Savern."

"Don't listen to him, good doctor," Eddie said, waving a hand in Hatch's direction. "He's just grumpy because Pip wrecked his car."

"That has nothing to do with this or my mood," Hatch said, indeed sounding more irritated than usual. "You are all throwing out impossible assumptions which are distracting you from finding out exactly what the Saverus are up to, or what will happen if they are successful. The size of the tear that planet would leave behind would be enough to split the galaxy in half. Nothing will survive it."

Julianna rolled one of her shoulders back, trying to ease the tension in her neck. "Hatch, I think you have the intention of trying, in your own weird way, to be helpful, but I'm not sure your approach is good for morale."

"That is an important topic, and I'm glad you've brought up," Jack stated, clearing his throat again. He gave Eddie and Julianna a hesitant look. "It hasn't gone unnoticed by me that stress is running high on the ship."

Hatch attached a wire to the end of the client, his focus

intent on the device. "That tends to happen when the crew is trying to stop a race of deceptive shapeshifters who could end us at any moment."

"I realize that," Jack stated with a confident nod. "Still, if we don't take care of ourselves, we're not going to be in a position to stop the Saverus."

"Spoken like a man regurgitating something Liesel would say," Hatch muttered, earning a small chuckle from Knox.

Jack cut his eyes at Hatch, releasing a steadying breath. "Although Liesel was the one who gave me this idea, I do speak as the Chief Strategist."

"Tell me, Jack…What happened to your slacks?" Hatch asked, sounding particularly cranky.

Jack looked down at his clothes. He did appear a little more casual than usual, in his woven, trim pants and loose button-down shirt, the sleeves rolled up to the elbows. "I thought I'd try something different. These are supposed to be breathable, which is good for your skin."

"For *your* skin maybe," Eddie said, diverting his eyes as he suppressed a grin.

Hatch puffed out his cheeks, his gaze still focused down. "I'm just glad you ugly humans cover your bodies in the first place."

"I bet you're glad *you* don't have to wear pants," Eddie said, letting out a deep laugh. "I mean, humans put theirs on one leg at a time, but Londils—"

"Shut up, Captain," Hatch groaned.

Jack coughed to clear the air. "Anyway, as I was saying.

I've had Ricky Bobby monitoring our stress levels, and he reports that they're at an all-time high. Therefore Liesel has volunteered—"

"And there we go," Hatch interrupted. "I knew she'd be behind this."

"As I was saying," Jack stated. "Liesel has put together some stress relieving techniques for the crew, and will offer them starting this evening."

Eddie laughed. "If you think I'm doing yoga, you've got another thing coming."

"No one wants to see you in yoga pants, or whatever that getup is that Jack is wearing," Hatch remarked.

"Amen, doc!" Eddie exclaimed.

Jack shook his head. "It's not yoga, although Liesel will offer those sessions in the morning, if she gets more requests."

"It's funny, I thought we recruited her to be the engineer, not the activity director," Hatch stated.

Eddie laughed. "She's quite the bargain."

"Anyway," Jack said again, trying to steer the discussion back on track. "Liesel is offering a Pinot's Palette class tonight in the lounge."

"A what?" Knox asked, looking up suddenly from the workstation.

Jack nodded with a smile. "Apparently, it's been proven to help people unwind and channel creativity. Liesel gave me some data suggesting that letting out creative steam improves morale. Ricky Bobby was able to back up her findings, so I'm confident this is a method worth trying."

"And yet we still don't know what it is," Eddie stated. "What's Pinot's Palette?"

"Wine and painting," Julianna said, her tone dull.

Jack shot her a smile. "That's right. Wine is shown to decrease stress hormones and lower blood pressure, putting artists more at ease. While you sip on a glass, Liesel will guide you through the process of creating your own masterpiece."

Eddie waved his arm forward, encouraging Jack to say more.

"That's it," Jack stated with finality.

"Where's the part when you say, 'Just fucking kidding'?" Eddie asked, his tone serious.

Jack shook his head, striding for the exit. "I'm not at all kidding. I take your mental well-being seriously, and don't want you overdoing it. I think this event is what you all need; a way to relax while also team building."

"We're busy working on the Tangle Thief," Hatch grumbled.

"Yeah, I'd love to, but I've got to help them with the Tangle Thief," Eddie joked.

"The hell you do!" Hatch exclaimed.

"I'd go, but I don't want to," Julianna stated blankly.

Jack sighed. "As you are the captain and the commander of this ship, I can't force you two to do anything. I can only give you the data showing that stress hormones are elevated in every single member of your crew. I hope you'll lead by example, though—you might not need this, but there are others on this ship who could benefit."

Julianna gave Jack an insolent expression. "Fine, I'll go, but I'm sipping whiskey, not fucking fruit juice."

"If she's going, I'll go too," Eddie agreed.

Jack beamed. "Good. I think you both made a wise decision," he said before turning and striding away.

"We've been had, you realize that, right?" Eddie asked Julianna.

"Yeah. Let's go grab a few bottles of whiskey," she said. "I need to get started early if I'm expected to hold a paintbrush and not use it as a deadly weapon."

Eddie looked impressed. "I'd actually pay good money to see that."

"I'd take your money," Julianna said as they sauntered away.

When the captain and commander were gone, Hatch's head snapped up. "Damn, I thought they'd never clear out!"

Knox let out a relieved breath. "Yeah, I was running out of ways to look busy with this thing." He pointed to the Tangle Thief.

"I already told them it won't lead us to the other parts of the device, but they don't listen." After a beat, Hatch's face brightened for the first time that day. "Ready to get to work on the DeLorean?"

"Hell yeah," Knox enthused. "I've got an idea for using cold fusion to bypass the problem we're having with fuel."

Hatch combed a tentacle over his chin. "Interesting. I'm not sure if that will work, but we can take a look."

Knox hopped up off his stool. "I left the plans in my room. I was working on it all night."

"All right, then," Hatch stated, waving the boy away. "Go get them while I pull out the tools."

Knox disappeared, leaving Hatch alone in his lab.

Jack was right about the crew's morale. For Hatch, it was at an all-time low. But working on the DeLorean was his Pinot's Palette...and doing it with Gunner helped.

Hatch was leaning over the engine of the DeLorean, trying to remember what they'd been working on last, when he'd been rudely interrupted by the group going on about Noah's ark. He shook his head at the ridiculous notion.

"I'm sorry," a muffled voice stated, yet another interruption.

Hatch pulled his head out from under the hood, straightening and listening intently. "What? Who was that?" he finally asked.

"Me," the familiar voice of Pip called from overhead.

Hatch's tentacles wound together tightly, their version of making fists. "Oh."

"I wanted to tell you that I'm sorry," Pip said, his voice uncharacteristically melancholy.

"For being a coward?" Hatch asked gruffly.

"For scratching your car," Pip stated.

"It's a bit more than a scratch!"

"I didn't mean to."

"That's what cowards say," Hatch seethed.

A long stretch of silence filled the space.

"I know you don't make mistakes," Pip finally said. "But maybe you can understand that, as someone new to emotions, and brand new to having access to a body, it's a bit much for me. I wasn't thinking, and allowed the thrill of the moment to get the best of me."

Hatch puffed out his cheeks, keeping his eyes low in an attempt to cover his own emotions. "I trusted you."

"And I let you down," Pip said, his tone subdued but still strong. "I understand that you're very disappointed in me and that earning back your trust will take time."

Hatch thought about dragging out Pip's misery with a round of insults, but the AI sounded more grown up than the mechanic had ever heard him.

"I wish you hadn't run off," Hatch finally said.

"As I am confined to the networks of the Etheric, we both know I can't run," Pip said without humor. "But you're right. I should have stood up like a man—I mean, like a man *or* a woman. Don't tell Julianna I said that first part. Anyway, I should have taken responsibility for my actions, which I intend to do now and in the future."

"Yeah, well, everyone makes mistakes," Hatch allowed.

"You don't," Pip reiterated. "I checked over your records for the last ten projects, and there wasn't even the slightest miscalculation. I can't imagine how hard it is for you to share space with the rest of us."

Pip sounded so unlike himself that suddenly all Hatch wanted was for things to return to how they were. "I'm no island," Hatch admitted. "I still need the rest of you, in order to do my job."

"I'd like to continue helping you with that, if you'll forgive me for making mistakes… although I can't guarantee it won't happen again," Pip said.

"You know what?" Hatch asked.

"What?"

"It's a sign of great strength when someone can hold their head up after making a mistake, take responsibility and learn something," Hatch offered.

"I'm not sure I was really good at holding my head up afterward, but I'll work on it," Pip stated.

"I'll help you."

16

Q-Ship, Cantijik Sea, Planet Sagano, Behemoth System

Lars flew the Q-Ship steadily over the turquoise waters of the Cantijik Sea, his eyes scanning the expanse that seemed to go on forever. Fletcher hadn't been still since he took the copilot's seat, but his nervousness was justified. His mission to stop Rosco had purpose now, whereas before it was simple revenge.

Vengeance had built empires and also turned them to dust. It was an emotion both productive and terrible. *Life is full of fine lines like that,* Lars thought. *Good and bad share a paper-thin fence.*

"There they are." Fletcher pointed to a group of four islands to the north. One was quite large, and the other three half its size.

"I bet Rosco's hiding on the biggest island," Nona said from the back.

"We'll have to fly over it to find out," Lars stated, cloaking the Q-Ship.

From their position, it was clear that the three smaller islands had suffered. Most of the trees were broken, and there were scorch marks on the soil. Several structures lay in ruin, and trash and debris were strewn a great distance from them.

"Whatever happened to those islands doesn't look pleasant," Nona observed.

"Maybe someone has already taken Rosco out," Lars mused hopefully.

It's not that he didn't want closure for his friend—it was more that he wasn't sure if this was the path to get it. The closer they got to Rosco, the brighter the scorching fire in Fletcher's eyes. Lars feared that his friend's need for retribution might burn him alive.

"I doubt it," Fletcher stated, narrowing his eyes at the islands. "The terrorist group he runs has been active, though aloof. We need to cut off the head of the beast… then we'll be one step closer to justice for all."

The larger island appeared untouched by the violent forces that had ripped the smaller ones apart. Two towers stood on either end, a lookout stationed in both. The vegetation stood tall and lush, and in the center of the island stood a large, open compound made of bamboo. It was flanked by guards holding automatic weapons.

"Looks like we found the base of operations," Nona stated, sitting up in her seat to peer out the windows.

Fletcher ground his fist into his palm, his teeth clenched. "Let's land on the beach on the far side of the island."

"I think…" Lars began, his tone careful, "we should

check out the smaller islands first. Find out what's happened."

"Rosco is obviously inhabiting the large island," Fletcher argued. "Why waste time when we know where to find him?"

"Because if he's responsible for the destruction of these other islands, we should find out what we're up against, collect some intel," Lars explained.

Fletcher stubbornly sharpened his gaze on the land mass ahead of them.

"I think Lars is right," Nona chimed in from the back. "I know you're anxious for this mission to be complete, but if we rush it, we could make a mistake."

Fletcher appeared to be on the verge of saying something, but only shook his head.

"The island looks incredibly well guarded, and we have small numbers," Lars said, calculating. "That's both to our advantage and disadvantage. I'm not worried about our chances of sneaking into the compound, but I'd like a bit more time to investigate."

"Hatch gave me two of the personal cloaking devices," Fletcher argued.

"Which sound great, but I caught the captain and commander while they were wearing them on a mission," Lars reminded him. "The cloaks aren't foolproof and they superficially inflate a soldier's confidence."

Fletcher chewed on his lip and softened a degree. "Yeah, you're right. Let's check out the smaller islands first."

"What about that one? It's populated, but from what I can tell, the habitants are civilian natives." Nona pointed, pulling her face away from her scope she'd been studying the islands through.

"Good work," Lars congratulated her, taking the ship in for a landing.

Fletcher knew that Lars and Nona were right, and he *had* recruited them for the mission because he respected their input. At his core, he knew he was too invested in killing Rosco, and that his hunger could be his undoing. That's why he'd let his teammates accompany him. He trusted Nona to keep him honest, and Lars to implement strategy.

The Q-Ship set down in one of the many clearings surrounded by scorched forest. In the distance, a child carried a pail of water away from the salty sea, her face and arms darkened from the sun. She wore a dress of torn rags, and her black hair was matted to her head.

"She's headed for the village over there," Lars said, catching Fletcher's line of vision. He pointed at a series of dilapidated huts on the higher end of the beach.

Why these natives didn't live inland, Fletcher couldn't reason. Staying close to the edge of the water wasn't just a risk, but being subjected to the unforgiving winds also made for uncomfortable living.

"What's the plan?" Nona asked, her eyes eager.

Fletcher strode toward the back of the ship where they stored extra supplies. He retrieved four warm blankets and handed them to Nona, who had been reaching for her rifle.

"Leave the guns behind," Fletcher stated. "Something

tells me that these people have seen enough guns to not trust those who wave them around freely."

When the Kezzin smiled, it made his face look strange, but it also suited him. "I would agree. Good instinct," Lars noted.

Fletcher pointed to two large containers of fresh water. "Can you carry those?" he asked Lars.

The pilot nodded, picking up the ten-gallon containers like they weighed nothing.

Fletcher pulled a large bag filled with rations and first aid supplies from the back of the storage unit, throwing it over his shoulder. "I say we bring these people gifts and earn their trust. Maybe then they'll tell us something useful about the large island."

"If nothing else, our offerings will mean a great deal to them," Lars reasoned with gentle pride.

———

A group of children looked up from a game they were playing in the dirt when the team of three strode in the direction of the camp. The settlement was small, consisting of only half a dozen small huts and a few larger ones. Women sat around a fire, some sorting through berries, others weaving. They looked up with alarm when the children hollered, running in their direction.

Fletcher faked a smile, hoping that the universal expression would tell the women that they weren't in danger.

One of the women stood, and her height was surprising. She had to be over six feet tall. Her shoulders were wide, but her hips narrow. The children all disappeared into one of the larger huts.

"What do you want?" the woman asked, her voice rough. Like the children, her clothes were threadbare, and her skin hung loosely around her eyes.

From the large hut the children now hid in, three men appeared, their expressions hostile.

"We mean you no harm," Fletcher stated, bowing. "We bring you gifts."

Nona set the thick blankets down in front of the tall woman and straightened, dwarfed by her height. She then darted her eyes to the water and medical bag that Fletcher and Lars had set down. Fletcher unzipped the bag to show the rich bounty within.

"Why have you brought this?" the woman asked, her chin raising high in the air.

"Because we are visitors to your land, seeking information," Nona stated.

The three men had come to stand beside the woman, and their eyes narrowed at the supplies.

"What is it you want to know?" the woman asked.

"What happened to your island, and what do you know about the larger island north of here?" Fletcher dared to say.

The wrinkles on the woman's face deepened. "Rosco happened, to this island and to our sister islands."

Fletcher let out a heavy sigh. "We feared as much. We're here to take him down, but we thought you might offer some insight."

The old woman measured him up with a penetrating stare. After a long moment, she put her back to him and strode for the fire. "Then come this way and make yourself useful. We labor while we talk, or the work never gets done."

Lars stared down at the bowl of nuts at his feet. Sitting awkwardly on the ground, he eyed the women around the fire, who were all regarding him with cautious glares. He knew he reminded them of Rosco simply because they were both Kezzin. They didn't know that many residents of Kezza were honest, hardworking farmers who desired a peaceful life.

Lars was reminded of a quote he had read that morning during his daily meditations. Stephen Hawking said, "The greatest enemy of knowledge is not ignorance, it is the illusion of knowledge." People thought they knew the Kezzin, based on their limited knowledge of the less attractive acts performed by some of the race, so they often underestimated the rest of them and held many biases.

Maybe in time, he could change that.

"Sort out the nuts from the rocks," the woman who had greeted them ordered. They'd learned her name was Vera.

Lars snapped back to himself and nodded, obediently pulling the bowl closer to him.

"You said that Rosco attacked the islands? Why?" Nona asked, sorting through a bowl of berries, her attention on the large woman.

Vera had taken a seat and gotten to work, weaving green vines. The men had moved off to the side to chop wood, but kept their eyes on the group.

"Because he's a power-hungry brute," Vera said. "For centuries, we've lived on these three islands, able to sustain a healthy balance by carefully borrowing resources from Anara, the main island, and the surrounding waters. We left Anara uninhabited and only took what we needed, even replanting the trees we chopped down. A year ago, Rosco set up a camp on that island. We confronted him, explaining how life in the Cantjik Sea is best preserved." Hostile outrage flared on the old woman's face as she wove more furiously.

Lars stared down at his bowl, realizing he hadn't been sorting. Nona, on the other hand, was almost through the berries, apparently having no trouble multitasking. It made him feel slightly better that Fletcher's hands were idle as he stared intently at their storyteller.

"He did not take your input thoughtfully," Fletcher guessed.

Vera shook her head. "He slaughtered many of our people and stripped our islands of valuable resources, then he burned them to the ground."

Lars sucked in a short breath, a nut cracking in his fingers from a burst of anger.

"I'm sorry," Nona said, bowing her head thoughtfully.

"I am too," Vera stated, her tone hot. "We are slow to rebuild, having lost so much and fearing his return."

"Which is why you live on the beach," Lars guessed,

gauging their proximity to the sea, where fishing boats were tethered.

Vera nodded. "We don't know another way. We can't survive another attack. Fighting him only leads to our end...We have to be ready to flee if and when he returns."

"Hopefully you will never have to," Fletcher stated, his words full of conviction.

"Do you know how many men he has around his compound?" Nona asked.

"Not many," Vera stated. "I've only ever seen a dozen or so men at any given time."

Nona looked to Fletcher hopefully. "Put me in a tree, and I can take out most of those men, especially with a diversion. Then you can get into the compound and get to Rosco."

Vera shook her head. "Rosco isn't in the compound."

"He isn't?" Fletcher asked, surprised.

"That's only where he keeps his stockpile," Vera explained. "He's in a cave on the northern tip of the island."

Lars smiled inside, grateful that they'd taken the detour to this island. They would not have thought to check the caves on their own, and Rosco would have had a chance to get away.

"That's really helpful," Fletcher said appreciatively, pushing to a standing position and wiping off his uniform.

"Do you think you three are enough to stop Rosco?" Vera asked, skepticism in her tone.

Fletcher smiled at Lars and Nona with pride before saying, "He'll never see us coming."

"Then I hope for all our sakes that you are successful," Vera said, her eyes dropping to the supplies they'd brought. "Thank you for the gifts. They will help more than you know."

"You're welcome," Fletcher replied. "And soon Anara will be yours once more."

Officer's Lounge, *Ricky Bobby*, Paladin System

Julianna took a sip of the red wine only to make Liesel quit looking her way.

"Doesn't it have a lot of complexity?" the engineer asked.

"Like a fucking crossword puzzle," Julianna sighed, and then tested the wine again. It wasn't whiskey, but it did have a boldness to it.

"Hey, Liesel Diesel," Eddie said, perched on his stool and shaking his wine glass at her. "Is this vino vegan?"

"It's made from grapes," Marilla said from his other side as she ran her paintbrush over the canvas. She hadn't even taken a sip of wine or whiskey, and was already busy painting a landscape of sunflowers.

She really doesn't know how this works, Julianna thought.

"But are they vegan grapes?" Eddie asked.

Jack, for all his pressuring, sat in the back row, where his canvas was out of sight. Julianna looked at her own blank canvas. She'd never dabbled in the arts—well, unless kicking ass was considered an art form. *She* believed it to be one.

"What you paint should be personal to you," Liesel instructed, striding through the easels with a carefree grin on her face. "If you need some inspiration, I have some art books at the front of the room."

I thought there was going to be a nude model, Pip said in Julianna's head.

She nearly jumped up out of her seat, she was so shocked and relieved to hear his voice. Instead, she put on her best indifferent tone.

Oh, hey.

Did you miss me?

Didn't realize you were gone.

He sighed. **Oh. I see that absence does not, in fact, make your heart grow fonder.**

Your mistake was thinking I had a heart.

You do. It's currently beating at seventy-two beats per minute. Maybe if I have the captain drop his brush and bend over to pick it up, your heart rate will increase.

Julianna nearly burst out laughing, but took a quick drink to cover it up. The red wine made her mouth pucker. This wasn't a drink she could slam.

Did you and Hatch make up? Did you beg for his forgiveness? she asked him.

Pleeeeease, he said drawing out the word. **I told him how it was, and he was like, 'Don't sweat a thing, Pip,' and I was all like, 'I don't sweat'. So yeah, we cool.**

Julianna's cheeks warmed as she suppressed another laugh.

"What's got you smiling?" Eddie asked, catching the look on her face.

She dabbed her brush in a glob of blue paint and spread it across the white canvas, making a dash of bold color. "Pip," she said simply.

"The little tyke is back?" Eddie asked, looking relieved and then hurt. "I haven't heard from him."

Tell him 'hoes before bros', Pip stated.

Julianna shook her head, dabbing her brush back into the blue paint. "He said he's afraid of the dark, and is therefore limiting his time in your head."

"Ouch!" Eddie said, clapping his hand to his chest.

Oh, good one.

Why haven't you said anything to Eddie yet? Julianna asked Pip.

I will, but I kind of figured I should re-establish contact with you first.

But you were using his body when you wrecked the car.

Scratched, he corrected. **And yes, but I'm...well, I guess I'm closer to you.**

We have spent a lot of time together, Julianna said, dabbing more blue on the top corner of the canvas, strangely enjoying the squishing sound her brush made.

I guess you could say that I missed you.

Julianna pulled the brush away, tilting her head to the side to regard her painting from a different angle.

Are you surprised to hear me say that? Pip asked.

Julianna smiled and took another drink of the bold, red

wine. She would be drinking whiskey, but she and Eddie had already finished the bottle.

Day drinking might be a problem at this rate, even with my nanos, she mused.

To Pip, she said, *I'm not surprised, but it's nice to hear you say it. I might have missed you too, but don't tell anyone,* she warned.

I've already blogged about it.

"Your picture…" Eddie began, and then hesitated. "It's a lot of blue."

Julianna stared at her canvas, a monochromatic rendition. "I like the color."

"It reminds me of a sky," Eddie said, dunking his paintbrush in yellow and drawing a circle on his canvas.

"Is that supposed to be a sun?" Julianna asked.

"Yeah, I figured I'd paint the thing I never missed but was always told I should," Eddie said, and for a moment, there was a rare depth to his tone.

"It's true that ship life doesn't give us much of a chance to see skies or suns, but we get a lot of time with the stars," Julianna said, looking out the bank of windows that offered a gorgeous view of a neighboring system.

The sun is also a star, Pip informed her.

Shut it. I thought it sounded poetic.

Leave the poetry to me, because bad poetry equals oh no-etry.

That's the worst thing you've ever said.

I'll try harder. I can do worse.

"What's Pip going on about?" Eddie asked. "You're grinning ear to ear."

"Oh, he's making no sense at all, so…the usual," Julianna stated.

"Tell him I said hi."

Tell the captain—

Pip, are you intentionally trying to be annoying? Julianna asked, cutting him off. *You can tell him whatever you like yourself, and you know that.*

I figured we could have some alone time.

Yes, just you and me and all these amateur painters.

Marilla's painting actually looks really nice. Chester's is kind of scary.

Julianna watched the hacker make black Xs on his canvas. *It's his own personal expression. Don't judge.*

The captain has made a cheerful sun, Pip observed.

Julianna gazed over to see an elementary sun on Eddie's canvas. It reminded her of something a child would paint with their fingers.

"Who are these people saying that you should miss sunsets and sunrises?" Julianna asked him.

He set down his brush and took a drink. "My mother."

"Oh," Julianna said, putting way too much blue paint on her brush.

She'd read Eddie's file and knew it by heart. His parents were huge supporters of the Federation, pilots who had served until the day they died, a notable and horrific day in history.

What Julianna didn't know was why Eddie blamed himself when, from everything she could see, he wasn't culpable.

"Yeah, she used to say that it was her love of the stars

that made her miss Earth," Eddie stated, a raw sincerity in his eyes.

"That's kind of beautiful," Julianna mused.

"*She* was beautiful. One of the most elegant women I've ever known," Eddie said softly, his paintbrush suddenly moving double-time as he talked. "She was strong but had a dainty femininity about her. My father absolutely loved her, and he of course adored that she was a pilot like him. They'd talk for hours about different maneuvers. She was smarter when it came to technique, but he was humbler. They were an incredible combination."

Sound familiar? Pip asked.

Julianna's brush swiped clear off the canvas, dripping blue paint on the floor.

You have the worst fucking timing in the world, she fumed, wanting to slap Pip.

Eddie stared down at the ground for a moment, seeming to collect his thoughts. Then he shrugged. "Anyway, sorry. I kind of went off, there. Didn't mean to."

"No, it's okay," Julianna said quickly. "I like hearing you talk about them."

Eddie paused, his paintbrush touching the canvas lightly as he stared at her, a slight, sideways smile on his face. "Thanks," he finally said. "I like telling you."

The two resumed painting in silence, listening to their own coarse brushstrokes like they were music.

18

Hatch's Lab, *Ricky Bobby*, Paladin System

From beneath the DeLorean, Hatch's tentacle appeared.

"I need a 9/16 wrench," the mechanic called to Knox.

A moment later, he heard soft-soled footsteps as his assistant went to fetch the tool. He didn't really need Knox to retrieve tools for him, but it made the repairs more collaborative.

This was something brand new for the Londil. In all his years, he had never really worked *with* anyone. With Cheng, he'd worked on one aspect of the Tangle Thief, while the doctor worked on the other. What he and Knox did was different. Better. He found himself whistling as the cold wrench was laid on his tentacle.

"Just another few bolts, and then I'll need you to crank her up," Hatch told Gunner as he took the tool.

"You got it," Knox said, his tone excited.

"Dr. A'Din Hatcherik," Ricky Bobby chimed overhead.

"I'm busy," Hatch said, his annoyance flaring.

"There has never been an instance when I've called on you that you weren't busy. I've never interrupted you unless it was important," the AI said.

Hatch wheeled out from under the car, inflating to his normal size. "What is it?"

"I've received a report that a radiation tear has been detected. It would appear that the Tangle Thief has been used again."

"Oh, dammit," Hatch cursed, tossing the wrench to the side. "Have you contacted the captain and the commander?"

"I have, and they, along with Dr. Sung, are already preparing to leave," Ricky Bobby said.

Hatch sighed. "Well, then, it sounds like it's all being taken care of. Why are you bugging me?"

"It was Dr. Sung's idea to alert you," Ricky Bobby informed him.

Hatch looked over at Knox, who was wearing a curious expression.

"Go on," Hatch urged.

"The Tangle Thief was used to steal quite a large supply of gold from inside a mine on Nexus," Ricky Bobby explained.

At first, this made no sense to Hatch...like he was working out a rare, unsolvable equation. Then the implications of such a theft, along with everything else he knew, became clear.

"I can't believe it," he said in a hush.

"That they used the Tangle Thief to steal riches?" Knox asked. "I can. That's what I would have used it for."

Hatch shook his head. "They don't want the gold for its wealth. They want it for its material properties."

Knox scratched his brow, looking perplexed. "I don't understand."

Hatch shook his head incredulously at what he was about to say. "I was wrong. The Saverus *are* building an ark."

Nexus, Tangki System

Eddie looked over his shoulder, keeping an eye out for any Saverus lurking nearby. Last time, they'd stayed behind to see who would come to clean up their mess, and he suspected they would do it again.

Cheng stumbled several times in the bulky, radiation-protective suit as he tried to get up the rocky cliff to the cave entrance. Although they'd parked the Q-Ship as close as they could, it was still a hike to where the tear was supposedly located.

When they reached the entrance to the cave, the bright light from the tear shone through the dark cave, illuminating every inch of the space. Eddie shielded his eyes as Julianna pulled out her sunglasses.

She's always prepared, the captain thought somewhat admiringly.

"This tear is quite a bit larger than the last one," Cheng said, motioning for them to back up.

"Well, they did steal the entire contents of a cave of gold," Eddie stated, still in disbelief over the theft.

It would have been impressive, if the effects weren't so

sinister. The Saverus were one step closer to their goal, which was not only terrifying, but infuriating.

Cheng fired on his vacuum gun, or whatever he called it—the guy didn't talk much or offer too many details. Eddie caught a hint of frustration in the doctor's movements after a moment.

"I'm not near enough!" Cheng yelled over the roar of the machine. "I have to get a bit closer."

"Be careful," Julianna warned, squinting from the brightness of the tear.

The ground was uneven and sloped dangerously in places. Cheng shuffled forward a few inches. His covered shoe caught on a rock, and he lunged forward, initiating a chain of stumbling steps, unable to catch his balance.

Julianna bolted after him, reaching for him before he could tumble down into the tear that threatened to swallow him whole. Her hands missed him, and he fell to the ground. He grabbed onto the rocks to stop his momentum, and the device in his hands clattered to the ground and rolled toward the opening.

Julianna dove after Cheng and clutched his wrist. She held onto him, trying to catch her breath, and after a few seconds, she tugged him toward her, encouraging him up.

Cheng looked over his shoulder to where the device lay. "My instrument!" he yelled over the whirling sound the tear made, like wind beating in a sail.

Julianna nearly yanked him over to where they'd been before his tumble, trying to keep him safe. "It's fine. I'll go get it."

Eddie shook his head. "No, you had an adventure just now. Let me do it."

Julianna glanced over to where the instrument had landed, only feet from the tear. It was bouncing slightly, like the vortex of the tear could pull it in at any second.

"Yeah, fine," Julianna agreed, handing him her sunglasses. "Wear these, though, or you won't be able to see."

"Thanks." Eddie took the glasses.

"And be careful," Julianna ordered. "If you get pulled in there, I'm not going in after you."

Eddie gave her a roguish smile as he eased past her. "Don't worry, boss. I'll be right back."

The suction of the tear quadrupled the moment he took a step forward, pulling at him with a strange intensity. Eddie felt like he was simultaneously walking against wind and being propelled forward. It was a bizarre feeling that he realized might mess up his movement, if he attempted to compensate for the competing forces in any way.

He crouched down low as he cleared the next few feet. The light from the tear was so bright it burned his eyes; a solar eclipse only yards away. A loud roar, like a train passing overhead, took over his hearing, blocking out all other noise. It felt like he was in the center of a tornado and was about to be thrown out of it.

Eddie lifted his foot, feeling an overwhelming pressure pulling it forward. He decided it would be best to crawl, and made to lower to the ground, but the vortex yanked him forward.

"Eddie!" Julianna yelled in panic.

The force dragged him several yards before he was able to anchor his weight and land on all fours. The tear was only five feet away now, the instrument within his reach. He extended his hand, his fingers brushing the edge of the device.

Inching forward with his face close to the rocky ground, Eddie gritted his teeth against the force spilling out of the vortex. He hoped his nanocytes were enough to hold up against the radiation blasting him in the face. *If not, I might as well let the tear swallow me up and spit me out who knows where.*

Again he reached out, extending his arm to its full length. His fingers bumped up against the instrument, knocking it farther away from him.

"Fuck me!" he yelled, the pressure on his face almost more than he could bear.

He took in a breath of what felt like cold wind and closed his eyes to the brightness. Operating on instinct, he placed his free hand under his chest for support and inched forward. His outstretched hand slipped around the handle of the device, but Eddie didn't allow himself a moment of victory. Instead, he yanked the instrument toward his chest and rolled back the way he'd come, pulling up to a standing position.

As he tried to retreat, the force drawing him backwards was even more compelling than before. He fought the slope of the cave, the vortex and the howling wind. Eddie picked up his leaden foot to move forward and knew immediately that he'd lose the battle. He whipped his head around, covering it with his arm, firmly believing he was about to plummet into the oblivion.

He slipped back several inches, but something caught his arm and, with an impressive amount of force, drew him forward.

Eddie strained around to find Julianna dragging him back up to the flatter ground of the cave, her breathing ragged. When he was a safe distance from the tear, she let him go and doubled over, heaving on each exhale.

"Thank you," Eddie said, his own voice hoarse. He handed the instrument to Cheng, who looked paler behind the hood of his suit.

"You nearly ruined my day," Julianna said, straightening.

"You're not done with me yet, Jules," Eddie said with a relieved wink.

19

Hatch's Lab, *Ricky Bobby*, Paladin System

"Do you want the bad news, the horrible news or the horrifying news first?" Hatch asked when Julianna and Eddie strode into his lab.

"I don't think you understand how this game works," Julianna said. "We're supposed to be given an option between good and bad."

"These are trying times," Hatch said, his face drawn. "If there was any good news to be had, I'd give it to you."

"I'll take bad news for two hundred, Alex," Eddie said.

Julianna shot him an incredulous look.

"What?" he asked, throwing his hands into the air. "It's a fucked up time; I almost got sucked into oblivion. We've got to try and make light of things, or we'll lose our spirit."

Ignoring him, Julianna returned her attention to Hatch. "What's the bad news?"

"According to my research, gold can be used to create a protective shield while transporting living organisms using the Tangle Thief," Hatch stated. "But you'd need an awful lot of it."

"Like a few tons taken from a mine?" Julianna asked.

"Yeah, that would do the trick," Hatch chirped reluctantly.

"So if the Saverus cover an entire building or ark or whatever it is that they have with gold, it will protect what's inside when they teleport Savern using the Tangle Thief?" Eddie asked.

Hatch shrugged. "I'm afraid so. I didn't think it was possible, but they appear to have found the solution."

"Which means that you were wrong when you said that there was no way they were building an ark and trying to transport animals," Eddie teased.

"And he was wrong when he said that there was no material that could protect living creatures being transported," Ricky Bobby stated overhead.

Hatch puffed up his cheeks. "So I made my first mistakes. Sue me."

"Why gold, though?" Julianna asked.

"Gold can't be corrupted the way other metals can," Hatch explained. "Its chemical structure is the least reactive."

"Are they really going to gold plate an entire structure or whatever it is that they need to take with them to Savern?" Julianna asked.

Hatch turned his attention to one of his workstations, checking the screen. "There are only thirty-five hundred species of life native to Savern."

"That's all?" Eddie asked, surprised.

"Only a select few can survive the hot climate," Hatch reasoned.

"Is anyone else surprised that the Saverus come from a planet likened to hell?" Pip asked overhead.

"There you are, little buddy. Where you been?" Eddie asked. "I've missed you."

"I've been busy working on my hedge fund portfolio," Pip answered.

Eddie rolled his eyes. He sensed that Pip, who had initially loved the idea of being paired with him, now felt a little strange about the whole thing. Maybe he felt like he was cheating on Julianna. Or maybe he didn't trust himself after the Corvette incident. Having a body was complicated, especially for an AI who was new to the whole thing.

"So all of the species on Savern could be housed in a manageable location?" Julianna asked Hatch, already thinking about their next move.

"It would still be sizable, but yes," Hatch confirmed.

"How hard is it to find a giant-ass warehouse that's being gold plated?" Eddie asked.

"About as hard as trying to find a four-leaf clover in a field of three-leaf clovers," Pip answered.

"So that's more of the horrible news," Eddie guessed.

Hatch shrugged. "I'm afraid so. The Saverus have everything they need to succeed. Now it's a matter of time before they execute their plan and steal Savern."

"And then what?" Eddie asked.

Hatch shook his head, his expression morose. "The tear would be too large to close, and it would suck us in one way or another. It wouldn't matter where we were."

Eddie remembered all too well how powerless he had been to resist the force of the tear created by the missing chunk of cave. He couldn't imagine the force of one large enough to fit a planet through.

Julianna let out a heavy sigh. "We have to keep searching. I'll go talk with Penrae. Maybe there's something she's overlooked. There has to be another option. Something we're missing."

The anxiety in her tone unnerved Eddie. He'd never heard her so flustered.

"There's something else," Hatch said, his voice careful.

"What?" Julianna asked, her eyes widening.

"It's relatively small in the scheme of things, but it's something that I thought you should know," Hatch stated.

"Go on," Eddie urged.

"The pet store from Onyx Station was located," Hatch said. "It was found on Savern."

"We can't find a giant warehouse being gold plated, but we were able to locate a small shop?" Eddie asked.

"It's a bit easier to find a place that materializes out of thin air," Hatch said, irritation heavy in his voice. "The Saverus were obviously just testing with the pet store, not overly concerned with its final location. My guess is that they had the gold sent to a place that wouldn't attract attention; the same goes for whatever location they've chosen for the ark."

"The animals?" Julianna asked, the unspoken part of the question hanging in the air.

Hatch blinked, looking away. "That's why they needed

the gold. The animals were all dead when the authorities found them."

Eddie pressed his eyes shut. It was only animals in a shop, but it was fucking *innocent* animals in a shop.

"Since we know what the Saverus are looking for," Julianna began, her words slow-coming like she was processing as she spoke, "Can we look for leads on Savern? Evidence of places where native animals and plants have been farmed for this ultimate goal?"

"That's a good idea, Julianna," Pip stated overhead. "I wish I had thought of that. Oh, wait...I did."

"Anything useful?" Eddie asked.

"There's a handful of leads, but the Saverus got a head start," Pip stated.

"Loop Penrae in on what you find," Julianna ordered. "She knows her people best and might see a clue we'd over-look. If we discover the facility, it might lead us to the Saverus."

"And if we find the Saverus, we can take back the Tangle Thief before they have a chance to use it," Eddie stated.

Julianna nodded back at him with pained conviction.

Anara, Cantjik Sea, Planet Sagano, Behemoth System

Fletcher knew exactly why Rosco had chosen the caves as his hideout. Not only would most enemies make the same mistake he did and think that the open compound was where Rosco was located, but the cave was also only accessible from the interior of the island. That meant they'd have to land the Q-Ship on the eastern side of the island and hike around. One entrance made the break-in even tougher—only one way in and out. Rosco operated with brute force, but Fletcher was going to take him out with stealth.

Nona activated her personal cloaking belt when the hatch door opened to reveal the jungle stretching out on the other side of the ship. She flickered for a moment and then disappeared.

"This is really bizarre," her disembodied voice said.

"Just remember that it's not foolproof," Lars warned, a sturdy expression in his eyes. "These guards may not be keen, but if they are alert, they'll hear you moving through the forest, or see the surroundings you displace, like the sand and leaves."

"I appreciate the heads-up, but I can handle it," Nona stated.

"She's like a cat; most targets never hear her coming," Fletcher said, a proud smile on his face.

"I'll be up that tree and ready on your mark." Nona's voice was confident, which Fletcher was glad for. Her position was crucial for this mission to be successful, and it all relied on timing.

"Okay, go on, then," Fletcher stated.

Nona chuckled over the comm. "I've already left the ship."

"Oh, right." Fletcher laughed and turned to Lars, holding up the other cloaking belt. "Are you sure you won't take this?"

Lars shook his head. "The point is that I need to be seen."

In truth, they'd reviewed the plan, and this made the most sense. It was frustrating, though, that there were only two cloaking belts. Life seemed to always be short one life preserver. It was a cruel joke.

"I'd still feel better if you could disappear after creating the diversion," Fletcher told him.

Lars wasn't on his team of special forces soldiers, he was a friend, volunteering for this mission. Therefore, Fletcher couldn't order him to do anything.

"Don't worry," Lars encouraged. "I'm excellent at running and blending in. I've been doing it my whole life."

Fletcher nodded. "Well, it's a big risk and it means a lot that you're doing this. Thank you."

"It's what friends do," Lars stated simply.

"I'm in position," Nona said over the comm.

Lars' mouth dropped open. "Damn. That was fast."

"I told you," Fletcher stated.

"How is it even humanly possible she got there so fast?" Lars asked.

"I'm not certain that Officer Fuller *is* human, actually," Fletcher said, fastening the cloaking belt around his waist. He offered Lars one last look of appreciation before activating the belt and disappearing.

It was much easier to hide when the goal was to be caught.

Lars was instantly transported back to his childhood, when he and his brother would play bounty hunter in the woods. He would pretend to be the fugitive, and Dequan would be the bounty hunter. Dequan would give Lars a fifteen-minute head start, but Lars didn't like the hiding part of the game as much as fleeing. He'd use his fifteen minutes to position himself in the perfect place to be found, giving himself the best advantage for escaping.

Dequan expected his brother to run deep into the forest to get a head start on him, so his surprise was always entertaining when he found Lars close by after his time was up. Dequan would find him waving from the opposite side of the ravine, or on the other side of the creek, which Lars would have to cross with cautious precision in the Spring months.

Now, Lars stayed low as he negotiated his way through the jungle on the island of Anara. Although he was Kezzin like Rosco's crew, he wasn't dressed the same as the guerilla members. He was dressed to blend in with his surroundings, even though the path he'd chosen was not easily visible from the cave or the compound.

Lars had studied the island from the cloaked Q-Ship, mapping out the best route as he watched the routine of the guards. It would have been easy to bomb the island from the safety of the ship, but they'd also be destroying the resources the natives desperately needed. Fletcher had promised the tribe that the island would go untouched, and Lars was going to help him keep that promise.

When he reached the large mound of boulders that lay halfway between the caves and the compound, he halted, putting his back against the rock and letting out a sigh of relief.

"I'm here," he said into the comm.

Fletcher couldn't believe how smoothly everything was going. Nona and Lars were both in place, and soon he would be, too.

The cave entrance was only twenty feet up a steep scree. Getting up there wasn't the hard part. The hard part was getting up there, cloaked, without alerting the two guards that flanked the entrance.

Fletcher chose a path that went to the left of the entrance. It involved a steeper climb, but it put him exactly where he needed to be—against the eastern facing side of the cave—and he wouldn't be in the guards' direct line of vision.

Listening to the distant mumbling of the guards, Fletcher searched for grips on the rock. There were plenty of cracks for him to wedge his toes into, but finding solid handholds was growing more challenging as he ascended.

Taking a shallow breath, Fletcher felt around the smooth section of the rock, trying to find something he could pinch onto. His father had taught him how to rock climb, and his words came back to him now. *'Every climb is merely a problem to be solved. There is always a solution.'*

Fletcher spotted a large grip to the left, a jug. If he could transverse over a bit, he would be able to pull himself up on it, nearly completing the crux of the climb. Using resistance, Fletcher pressed his hand into a slate of rock and pinned his toe to the same piece. He shoved off, suspended in air for a moment before his left hand caught the hold. His feet flailed in the air for a few seconds, attached to nothing. Fletcher brought his other hand around on the jug and lifted his body up, finding footholds.

With sweat pouring down into his eyes, he paused, taking small sips of air. Fletcher wiped his forehead against his shoulder and glimpsed the view beneath him. His breath caught in his throat. *Looking down is always a mistake.* The ground seemed to taunt him from thirty feet below. He hadn't realized how far he'd come, or how high the cave was from this angle.

Shoving away his fear, Fletcher pushed off the jug with one hand, reaching for his next handhold. He only had a few more feet to go until he would be on the wide ledge that ran around the cave.

The jug shifted under his hand. Fletcher jolted, falling a few inches. His feet scrambled against the rock, looking for a safer hold. With great effort, Fletcher pressed off the jug and caught a new grip. The rock broke away as the force of his weight left it, and he watched it tumble past his feet and roll down to the ground.

"What was that?" one of the guards called out in alarm.

Fletcher looked up to see the two guards hurrying around the side of the cave, looking his way. If he weren't cloaked, they'd be staring straight at him. With both of his hands required to hold onto the rock, Fletcher was a sitting duck. If they spotted him, they'd open fire, and he'd fall to his death. He had to hope the cloaking belt didn't fail right then.

Cementing his body to the rock, Fletcher tried not to even breathe, counting the seconds as the guards scanned the area.

"Loose rocks is all," one of the guards finally said.

"Come on, it's almost time for break," the other said, waving his partner back to the entrance.

Fletcher exhaled in relief and heaved himself up onto the ledge, not making a sound. When he'd regained his composure, he straightened fully.

"I'm in position," he whispered over the comm.

Lars checked his watch. They had three minutes until the two guards from the compound would cross by this rock structure on their way to relieve the guards at the cave entrance. *Plenty of time to climb up to the top of this boulder and give these guerillas a little show.*

"The guards are leaving the compound now," Nona reported over the comms.

"What?" Lars whispered. "They're early."

"You can do it," Nona encouraged, her voice a hush.

Fletcher couldn't say anything, Lars knew, since his position was the trickiest—right outside the cave entrance.

"Yeah, I've got this," Lars assured, and he scrambled faster, over the side of a large rock, diving for the one above.

It was an easy climb, just a series of large steps. He only hoped that the descent would be as easy.

"I'm here," he said over the comm when he was crouched below the peak.

From this angle, the guards in the lookout tower on the south end could spot him.

"The replacements are passing your location on the ground in three, two…now," Nona stated, her voice an excited hush.

Lars popped up and jumped onto the boulder. He stared down at the trail below, roughly twenty feet down. Two guards were marching along the path, heading for the cave entrance in the distance. From his vantage point, he could spot the guards stationed there, which meant they could see him, too. He tensed, looking around.

Being bait was incredibly nerve-wracking when the fish weren't biting.

The guards continued striding for the cave, too involved in their conversation to look up. The guards positioned by the entrance were focused on something to the side of the cave.

"Alert! Intruder!" the lookout from the tower yelled.

"Finally," Lars breathed.

The guards on the ground whipped their heads up, narrowing their eyes at the sight of Lars. The ones by the cave entrance reacted immediately, scrambling down the side of the rock and nearly slipping in their pursuit.

The lookout, having been shot, fell from the top of the tower, as Lars wheeled around and leapt off the boulders. He landed with a hard *thud*, rolling before stopping his momentum.

He sprinted through the jungle, not at all trying to be stealthy, leaves and vines slicing at him as he passed. He only needed to outrun these thugs and make it back to the Q-Ship in time.

Only a little farther, he told himself, pushing forward on his toes, nearly blinded by the thick vegetation he passed in a blur.

The compound had broken out in complete chaos.

The guards backed up, finding refuge inside the structure, which made it impossible for Nona to pick off any more of them. She'd taken out both lookouts from her place high in a tree. Then when Lars had been spotted, she had knocked off the two brutes standing on either side of the compound. That left two more, but they had retreated inside the open shelter.

Nona swung down from the tree, landing low on the sandy ground. She pulled her gun from its holster, keeping her weapon steady as she scanned the darkening forest. The compound had fallen silent.

The cowards are hiding. That was fine by her; she was excellent at this game, especially cloaked.

Striding toward the entrance, Nona checked over her shoulder. *Lars should be back at the ship by now.*

"I'm in," Fletcher stated over the comm.

Everything is going according to plan so far, Nona thought, entering the cool shade of the structure.

The thatched roof was held up by large support beams, and mesh nets hung from the rafters. In the center, stacked crates formed a makeshift room, but didn't reach all the way to the ceiling.

Sliding her back along the first wall of crates, Nona stepped sideways, pausing when she came to a corner. She peeked around the pillar of crates, and caught movement on the other side of the compound. A Kezzin was fleeing, setting off to the west where the ships were docked. He was almost too far to reach.

Nona holstered her pistol, pulling her sniper rifle off her back and quickly taking aim. She fired once, shooting the retreating Kezzin in the back, and he fell flat. She lowered her rifle, feeling pride growing in her chest at the quick kill.

Behind her, she heard a click.

Lars could smell the salty air of the ocean. Light filtered through the leaves as he progressed, the jungle thinning. *Only a few more yards.* He burst out into the open air of the beach and halted.

Two Kezzin holding rifles stood in front of him, blocking his path to the cloaked Q-Ship.

"Hands up!" one of them ordered.

Lars' hands twitched by his sides. He was fast, but he wasn't sure if he was quick enough to outmaneuver both guards.

"I'm lost," he lied. "Me being here is an accident."

"An accident?" one of the Kezzin growled. He pointing at the closest tower using his rifle. "Is it an accident our men were killed?" The Kezzin's eyes were hollow.

Lars knew they were murderers, but there was something supremely sinister about these two.

Lars' fingers twitched by his gun.

"Take off your boots!" one of the brutes said.

"You got the boots the last time," the other complained.

"And I'm getting them this time."

Lars decided these weren't the type to negotiate with.

He shot his head to the side, like he'd heard a noise beside them. As he intended, this caught the attention of both guards, momentarily distracting them. When they checked over their shoulders, he reached for his gun and yanked it up, firing off a shot at the closest Kezzin.

The pirate flew back, nearly knocking into the cloaked Q-Ship. The other Kezzin fired in response.

A stabbing pain shot through Lars' shoulder, and he went soaring backward from the close-range assault. His gun fell to the sand with a muffled *thud*. Clapping his hand over his injured shoulder, he coughed, feeling an obstruction in his airways.

"Now I'll have to take the boots myself," the pirate said, aiming his weapon at Lars' head.

He couldn't believe this was how it was going to end— looking down the barrel of a gun, and one of his own, a fellow Kezzin, about to pull the trigger.

―――――

Nona stiffened, her finger moving back over her trigger. She had only one option.

Dropping her body weight, she ducked and slid around the corner of the crate, getting behind cover. Gunshots zipped by, too close for comfort. She spun, angling her rifle around the side of the crate, and fired at a figure. She was too late; he had slid back behind the crates on the other side.

Fuck!

Although she was still cloaked, this Kezzin knew her location. Thankfully, she also knew his.

A shuffling noise caught her attention, but Nona couldn't tell if the pirate was coming around from the left or the right. *Actually, it sounds like it's overhead.* She looked up at the ceiling to spy only open rafters and the backside of the thatched roof.

Then she remembered that the crates behind her didn't reach all the way up to the ceiling. Nona spun around, her rifle at the ready.

Pulling himself up onto the top crate, roughly fifteen feet off the ground, was the Kezzin. He surveyed the ground, trying to locate Nona's cloaked form.

She took a step back, considering how to handle the enemy. *Maybe I can disarm and restrain him...*

Then the Kezzin pulled an automatic weapon from behind his back.

Where the fuck did that come from?!

He pointed the gun at the ground, a vengeful menace on his face. This pirate wasn't taking any chances.

Fueled by preservation and directed by instinct, Nona aimed at the Kezzin and fired once, hitting him straight in the chest. He stumbled back a step and fell over the side of the crates, crashing to the ground.

Nona took a deep breath to steady herself, but the sound of gunfire in the distance stole the moment she had to refresh.

Lars!

She bounded for the jungle.

When the guards at the entrance to the cave were pulled in Lars' direction, Fletcher slipped inside. He could have shot them to gain entry, but it was best if Rosco got as little warning of the attack as possible. As it was, these goons would be in radio communication with each other, which meant Fletcher had to be fast.

The cave was lit by fire, and the tunnel was surprisingly wide. Fletcher blinked as his eyes adjusted. Ahead, he could make out the back of a rather large Kezzin, easily taller than Lars. The pirate reached for the radio receiver that was squawking on his belt.

This is it, Fletcher thought. *The communication that will send everything into chaos.*

"What's that?" the Kezzin said into the radio.

A voice crackled from the other end, the perfect cover for Fletcher's footsteps.

"Did you say 'invasion'?" the Kezzin asked.

Fletcher pulled a length of wire from his pocket, readying himself.

"There's a sniper—" The voice cut out.

"Nacha?" the Kezzin asked. "Nacha, where'd you go?"

Fletcher said a silent prayer as he swung the wire around the Kezzin's head. When it was at the large alien's throat, Fletcher yanked with all his strength, pulling his target backward.

The pirate's arms flew into the air, and a gurgling sound echoed from his mouth.

Fletcher nearly flew back from the weight of the Kezzin pressing against him, but was able to secure their position beside the cave wall. He tightened his grip on the wire and yanked again.

The pirate fell still.

Fletcher allowed the Kezzin to slip from his grip, quietly depositing him on the ground. He was a little surprised that he'd been able to take down the much larger alien.

"What?!" a voice boomed from nearby. "Not on my island!"

Fletcher let out a hot breath. He'd imagined this moment for years…The chance to face his father's murderer. Each time, it ended in blackness. Fletcher could never visualize how he'd finish Rosco.

He took a step forward, eager for what came next.

Lars always thought he'd close his eyes when faced with his death. It surprised him that he now blinked back at his would-be murderer, not even flinching as he stared up the length of a gun. The pirate sneered down at him, no decency in his eyes, as Lars lay in the sand, injured and bleeding.

A shot rang through the air.

Lars thought he was numb, and that the bullet had ripped through him, about to end his life. *Maybe I'm in shock. Maybe, in death, there is no pain.*

He pulled his eyes away from his murderer's to look at his torso, where he expected to see a fresh wound. There was nothing.

The goon in front of him screamed and dropped his gun. Lars couldn't understand why there was a bright, crimson stain blossoming across the pirate's shirt in the center of his chest, growing fast.

Slapping his hand over the wound, the brute fell to his

knees, confusion written on his face.

Lars pushed up onto his hands, though his shoulder screamed from the effort. He shuffled backward as the guard fell forward, landing on his face.

Behind him, standing like a warrior returning home to find their land pillaged, stood Nona. Her face was contorted in a fierce expression. At the sight of Lars laying wounded, she sprinted forward.

"Are you okay?" she asked.

"Yes, I'll be fine thanks to you," Lars said, grimacing as he tried to stand.

Nona helped him up, checking over her shoulder for more guards.

"Did you get them all?" Lars asked, leaning on her a bit more than he liked.

"That was the last one on the ground," Nona stated, opening the cloaked Q-Ship. "All that remain are the ones in the cave."

Fletcher slid around the corner, his back firmly pressed against the cave wall. In the next room, the firelight was brighter.

"What do you mean no one is answering?" Rosco yelled.

"I don't know, sir," a voice said. "I can't explain it."

"Well, go out there and see what's happening," Rosco ordered. "If it's those damn tribespeople, I'll roast them over their own fires tonight!"

Footsteps drew closer. Fletcher threw out his arm as

the Kezzin came around the corner, knocking the goon in the throat. Fletcher reached his other arm around the guard's neck and pulled out his gun, pointing it forward. Grateful this Kezzin wasn't as large as the one he'd just killed, Fletcher pushed his catch forward, using his body as a shield.

Rosco had heard the assault and was holding up his gun, pointing it straight at Fletcher when he came into view.

"What do you want, human?" Rosco yelled, his voice full of laughter.

"Put down your gun," Fletcher demanded, his eyes narrowing at the vermin before him.

Rosco didn't look too different from most Kezzin. Maybe overfed a bit, and with a special bitterness in his eyes, but otherwise, he had all the same features.

He laughed and shot once, hitting the Kezzin in Fletcher's grasp.

The alien yelped in pain, trying to reach for the wound in his abdomen. His weight and the force behind the impact of the bullet nearly made Fletcher double over. He threw the Kezzin to the ground, seeing him now as more of a liability than a shield. The guard cried out in pain, trying to say, 'Why?'.

Looking rather annoyed, Rosco fired at the Kezzin again, killing him. Fletcher was prepared for that and used the opportunity to fire at Rosco, knocking the gun from his hand. He could have shot him dead right then, but he needed to tell this Kezzin why he had hunted him down.

He needed to see Rosco's face when he explained why he was ruining him.

Rosco growled and dropped his gun, waving his injured hand like it was on fire. "*You!*" he said viciously.

"You killed your own man," Fletcher said, aiming straight at the Kezzin's heart.

"He knew it was a possibility when he signed up," Rosco said, his voice deep and rough.

"When you enslaved him," Fletcher corrected.

Rosco smiled, not seeming at all put off by being forced to stare at the barrel of someone else's gun.

"I know all about you," Fletcher began. "You take these men when they're young. You tell them that you saved them from something, but really it was you who murdered their family or burned their village to the ground or stole everything they owned. It's you they should be running from, but none figure it out until it's too late. You force these men to work for you, and none of them know the truth."

Rosco reached for something at his waist. Fletcher fired again, shooting the pirate in the foot.

"You motherfucker!" Rosco yelled. "How dare you come here?! What do you want?"

"Everyone on this island is dead," Fletcher informed him. "You're about to join them."

"What did I do? Take your treasure? Steal your home?"

There was no remorse in Rosco's voice. Fletcher's hand shook.

"You killed my father."

An evil laugh ripped from Rosco's mouth as he hopped

on one foot, blood spilling from the hole in his boot where his foot was wounded. "Join the club, you sappy human. I kill. That's what the Kezzin do. Get over it."

Fletcher aimed his gun to the left and shot again, the loud bang echoing off the cave walls. The bullet shot through the fleshy part of Rosco's bicep; he had more flesh than most Kezzin, and he screamed again, clapping his hand over his arm.

"That's not what Kezzin do," Fletcher corrected. "That's what *you* do, you fucking worthless maggot, fucking piece of shit." He was suddenly flooded with emotion, like the dam he'd built all those years ago when his father died had suddenly burst open.

"Fine!" Rosco yelled, his voice raw with physical pain. "You want to kill me? Kill me! Do it now! Get the revenge you came for."

Fletcher aimed at the alien's heart.

All he had to do was pull the trigger, and it would all be over. He'd made Rosco suffer, as he'd intended. He'd told him what he came here for. And Fletcher saw with his own eyes the despicable savage who had murdered his father.

And yet, he couldn't bring himself to end him. There was something stopping him. Something telling him that there was another way. A different path his father would have wanted for him.

"Rosco, you are under arrest for the murder of Cornell Fletcher, as well as for many other crimes," Fletcher intoned, disbelieving what he was saying.

"What?" Rosco asked, sounding grossly alarmed by this news.

"You'll be tried and sentenced for your crimes, because death is too kind an end for you."

"No!" Rosco yelled, blood oozing down his arm. "No, just kill me."

Fletcher wasn't sure why he had done it, but this was the right option; he knew it with such certainty. He didn't automatically feel lighter, though, as he thought he would. He realized it would take more than revenge for him to get over his father's death, but he also knew he hadn't come for revenge. He'd come for justice.

An intuition as ingrained in him as his father's love told Fletcher that he would get it. Apprehending Rosco would bring about justice for thousands, not just for Fletcher.

Jack's Office, *Ricky Bobby,* Tangki System

Fletcher kept his eyes low and his elbows pinned on his knees as Eddie paced the room. Julianna stood stoically nearby, as usual.

"What do you think Jack meant when he said, 'this could change everything'?" Eddie asked.

Fletcher shook his head, feeling the space between his thoughts evaporate a little more. His head was feeling increasingly crowded.

The look on Nona's and Lars' faces when Fletcher marched Rosco onto the ship had made him question his decision.

Twice, he'd held his gun to the pirate's head, but each time something deep within him told him he didn't want the alien's blood on his hands. Fletcher was trained to kill. He was practiced at handling the complexity that came with ending a life. However, he couldn't kill Rosco—the one person he'd been dreaming of hunting down for *years*.

Life was weirdly ironic.

The captain and commander were even more surprised than Nona and Lars were when they found out Rosco was locked up in the brig of *Ricky Bobby.* Jack, who hadn't known about the side mission at all, was totally stunned when he got the news. He took off for the brig with an exclamation, sprinting through the corridors, his suit jacket flying behind him.

Since then, they'd all been sequestered to Jack's office, with no information and a lot of quiet time to ruminate.

"What was Rosco into?" Julianna asked, not answering Eddie's question about Jack.

Fletcher shrugged, looking up at the two of them. "He was a dirty pirate."

Eddie gave him a worried stare. "We both know he was more than that. He worked with the Nihilists. This was a Kezzin who was out for more than riches and power. Rosco interacted with the foulest of creatures. He does not have a soul."

"How does it get worse than the Nihilists?" Julianna asked, shivering from the idea.

Fletcher knew she'd seen some things in her many years, but nothing was worse than a group of beings who had no concern for life.

"I can think of a worse bunch. I'd still lump them as a group of greedy pirates, though," Eddie reasoned.

"Yeah, I guess they're not as bad as selfish shapeshifters who are willing to sacrifice billions to get their planet back," Julianna agreed.

Fletcher had momentarily forgotten about the mission to stop the Saverus, so thick was his hate for Rosco.

Eddie combed his hand over his forehead. "We will get a lead on that, don't worry," he said, his voice hypocritically full of anxiety.

Julianna nodded, a numb expression on her face.

"How is Lars?" Fletcher asked, trying to fill the silence.

Eddie smiled. "He's fine. Well, he always says he's fine, but even the doctors agree that he will be all right. Just needs a little bit of rest."

Fletcher nodded, his head heavy. He knew that Lars had signed on for the mission, but it was still hard for him to think that his friend had been injured while on Anara. When he and Nona had transported Lars to the medical wing, he hadn't acted like he was in pain at all.

Instead, he couldn't stop talking about how the natives of the Cantjik Sea could go back to a life of peace, now that their mother island was returned to them. This had brought pride to Fletcher, too—knowing they'd done more than apprehend a deadly pirate.

As they helped Lars to a bed in the infirmary, he swayed, watching them with a dazed look in his eyes. "It's not a happy ending for those natives. It's better. It's a happy beginning."

Then the Kezzin's eyes rolled back in his head, and he passed out from blood loss.

After ten more minutes of silence, Jack burst into his office, his attention on his desk.

"What's going on?" Julianna asked, though he'd dashed right for his computer and began typing furiously.

He slammed his finger down on a final key, eyeing the screen. Something popped up on the monitor a moment later.

Jack's eyes broadened, excitement springing to his face. "Yes! That checks out!"

"What checks out?" Eddie asked, striding over to the desk.

"I got Rosco to talk," Jack stated simply, crossing his arms in front of his chest.

"About...?" Julianna encouraged.

Jack strode around his desk, taking a seat on the arm of one of the chairs. "It's only a small lead, but it's better than anything we've had in ages, and I suspect it will lead to more information."

Julianna lowered her chin, staring at Jack with hooded eyes. "Specifically, what the hell are you talking about?"

Jack, who appeared more than lost in his excited thoughts, nodded, seeming to try to come back to himself. "Right, sorry. It's only that we've been grasping for leads, and this is a huge breakthrough." He shook his head, realizing that he was going off on another vague tangent. "Anyway, I've known for a while that Rosco was working with a group called the Starboard. However, as you three know full well, tracking down Rosco was near to impossible. Good work, there, Fletcher."

Fletcher released a hesitant smile, nodding his acceptance of the compliment.

"So you've been hunting for this group, Starboard?" Eddie asked.

Jack shook his head. "No, I've been looking for the corporation they serve."

"Oh, right!" Eddie chirped. "Because they are the villains responsible for a terrorist organization or weapons dealer."

Jack shook his head again. "No. The corporation, although corrupt, is only a small powerhouse. They have a partnership with a truly horrendous corporation, which continues to evade prosecution for their evil deeds."

"Got it!" Eddie stated. "And Rosco's lead gets you one step closer to this corporation."

"But the corporation isn't the end goal here," Jack said.

Eddie laughed. "Of course not. Why didn't I see that this rabbit hole would just keep going?"

Jack cleared his throat. "Monstre Corp is responsible for the degradation of a cluster of planets on the Frontier."

"Why aren't we out there stopping them?" Eddie asked.

"Because you're here, trying to stop the Saverus," Jack stated simply. "There are many battles to be fought."

"And with this lead, we're one step closer," Julianna concluded firmly.

Jack agreed with a nod. "Monstre is only as bad as its leader. A man named Solomon Vance. If that name doesn't inspire fear in you yet, it will once you become acquainted with his history."

"So he uses his corporation to intimidate the Frontier, all the while going unchecked, is that right?"

"Pretty much," Jack confirmed. "We can't even locate the board members, much less Solomon. The corporation's dealings are always quick, so by the time we get wind of it, they've disappeared to another area of the Frontier."

"Sounds like Ghost Squadron needs to put a swift end to this bullying organization," Eddie said.

"Although Monstre Corp is a big part of the problem," Jack began, "the organization isn't the reason that Solomon is dangerous. The threat is that he used to work within the Federation as a scientist."

Eddie let out a loud breath. "It's always the science-types who are the most diabolical."

"I don't disagree," Jack said with a laugh. "Science is the most radical power. It changes everything."

"What did Solomon do to get thrown out of the Federation?" Julianna asked.

"He didn't get thrown out. He left," Jack said, dark shadows flicking in his eyes. "Taking with him a specimen, and all the research for the project he'd been working on with his team."

"We have backups, though," Julianna argued.

Jack shook his head. "Solomon was thorough. He didn't leave anyone alive who could speak about the project."

"He killed his team?" Eddie asked, disgust heavy in his voice.

Jack nodded darkly. "I'm afraid so."

"Then we have no way of knowing the details of the project or the specimen," Julianna stated.

Jack rose, leaning forward on his toes, and clasped his hands behind his back. "It's true that we know little, but what we do know is that, if his project was successful, he could be more powerful than almost anyone in the Federation. It was rumored that he'd found a way, using the Etheric, to bring a collective energy to life, to harness an all-encompassing power."

"I-I-I don't understand," Eddie stuttered. "Why would that be considered?"

Jack let out a breath. "Solomon was trying to create a monster."

Julianna shot Eddie a cautious look. *Humans and aliens are monsters. We create ships and weapons to fight our battles with. How is this so different?*

"It's impossible to tell at this point if Solomon was successful," Jack began, "but if he was, this monster could soon be loose. There's no telling what it is capable of, but, based on Monstre's history, we won't want to find out the hard way."

"So your lead checked out?" Eddie asked, pointing at the computer screen.

"Yes, but it only leads to Starboard," Jack stated. "There's still a lot of digging and hunting to be done."

"We wouldn't even have that, if Fletcher hadn't brought Rosco in for trial," Julianna stated, nodding proudly in his direction.

He had sat quite still throughout the meeting, stress making his shoulders tense.

Jack smiled broadly. "It's the biggest break we've had in a long time. Great work, Lieutenant."

"We're ready to start hunting for this Solomon," Eddie said, all fired up.

Jack swallowed and nodded. "In time. Right now, the Saverus should be our priority."

"Right," Julianna said, striding for the door, before remembering they still had no leads on the case.

It was infuriating.

The ship shifted slightly, buzzing with the familiar vibration that happened right before they gated.

The commander froze. Then she turned and looked at Jack. "Did you request a change in our locations? Is there new information on the Saverus?"

His face scrunched up in confusion. "No, I have no new information."

"I've taken it upon myself to change the location of the ship," Ricky Bobby stated overhead.

"Why?" Julianna asked, irritation flaring in her voice. "We agreed that being close to Savern was best, in case we need to move fast."

"That's correct, but I've made a different decision based on my own observations," Ricky Bobby said.

"What's going on?" Jack asked.

"The team currently has no breakthroughs in the case, and meanwhile, morale and stress continue to be a negative factor for the crew," Ricky Bobby explained.

"That's because we are up against a tight deadline," Julianna argued, her voice rising. "If we aren't in position when something happens, how can we stop it? So much is riding on us to stop the Saverus. You get that, right, Ricky?"

"I absolutely understand," Ricky Bobby said, unaffected by the scolding.

"Then why would you take us away from the planet?" Eddie asked.

"Sometimes a break can lead to a bit of clarity," Ricky Bobby stated. "I made the executive decision that you and the crew needed something to help break through the walls. Because if you stay positioned where you are, you may never get any closer to learning what the Saverus are up to, and then you'll be at the epicenter of the tear."

"How dare you!" Julianna revolted. "You can't make executive decisions."

"I can, actually," Ricky Bobby said matter-of-factly. "And I firmly believe that where I'm taking you will help. What the team needs is a break, so that you can make a break through. Then you'll be ready to pursue the Saverus."

Julianna pressed her eyes closed. It made sense, but it also meant taking a giant risk.

She let out a steadying breath, trying to quell her anger. "I hope you're right, Ricky Bobby."

"My instinct tells me that I am," he said.

"Okay, so where are you taking us?" Eddie asked.

"It's a surprise," Ricky Bobby stated simply.

22

En route to Planet Noircun, *Q-Ship*, Tangki System

"What do you suspect is down there?" Eddie asked over the comm as he steered one of the six Q-Ships down to the planet below.

"Probably not enough whiskey to save Ricky Bobby's ass," Julianna sent back. She peered through the viewscreen at the glowing blue and green planet. It didn't appear especially unique, except for the splashes of pink and purple lights that sparkled and faded every so often.

"I ask that you keep an open mind, Julianna," Ricky Bobby said, interfaced into the comm for this team-building mission.

"People only ever say that when they realize they're about to disappoint," Julianna said to Harley, who sat in the copilot's seat. The dog gave her a sideways look that she instantly interpreted as agreement.

"My initial scans of the terrain aren't picking up

anything of unique interest," Marilla reported from the first row behind Julianna.

"There could be several plausible explanations for that," Chester reasoned.

Marilla shrugged, continuing to type on her device.

Julianna let their musings fade into a soft mumble in the background as she stared at the ships around her. It was hard to believe that a few months ago, they'd had only one Q-Ship, and the team was only her and Eddie.

"We've come a long way," Julianna said absentmindedly to Harley.

He scanned the ships in formation around them— seeming to read her mind—and whimpered, a soft, agreeable sound.

I should be jealous of the easy relationship you have with the dog, Pip said in her head.

Because... Julianna probed.

Because he gets you more than I seem to, he complained.

You started off as an irritating EI and slowly evolved into an even more annoying AI.

And Harley was once a slobbery dog who licked his ass, but now understands what you say and responds accordingly...but has no formal education.

Your point?

You seem to click with him.

I click with you, she argued.

No, we like each other, but there isn't the same chemistry.

What are you talking about?

You and I have a love-hate relationship.

I hated Harley at first.

Only because you were afraid of loving him. Just like someone else I know...someone who has no formal education, but who has evolved.

Your insinuations aren't appreciated.

Do you think you'd ever have truly loved Harley if you hadn't had to risk everything to save him? Pip mused, a playful tone in his voice.

Do you have a point?

Love is a bed of hot coals one must walk across.

That makes no sense.

Pip sighed. **I know. I don't feel like I make much sense lately.**

Huh. Sounds rough, Julianna said, entering the planet's atmosphere.

I know, I'm concerned too.

I'm sure it's nothing. Try not to worry about it, she said dismissively.

I'd love to talk about it more with you later. Thanks.

Julianna smiled. *I'm busy later.*

After a moment she said, *If I'm honest, though, you sound restless, Pip.*

How observant of you. I'm shocked.

I've had experience with these things.

Well, what do you think is going on, at my core?

I think that you are going through another mini evolution. Maybe it started when you entered the captain's head, or took over his body. Or maybe it's stemming from something different. The thing is, Pip, that when we think we have everything all figured out, the landscape changes, and we realize that we still have so much to learn. I could live a thousand lifetimes and still not know everything.

You know, Julianna, despite your bad temper and preference for hairy men and hairier creatures, I really like you.

You know, Pip, you're an asshole, but I kind of like you too.

Okay, I'm going to go look at my horoscope and see if it will shine any light on this situation.

How do you have a zodiac sign?

If I'm going with my evolution to AI, that makes me a Ophiuchus.

What? That's a sign? I've never heard of it.

Oh gods, Jules. Get with the times. They added a thir-teen sign eons ago to accommodate the thirteen constellations.

As seen from Earth.

So…?

So I guess Ophiuchuses aren't known for their logic, then?

We are the bearer of serpents.

Well, that should prove useful in our battle against the Saverus, Julianna joked.

We are also sexually alluring and jealous lovers.

I just threw up in my mouth.

Hiss, Pip said as Julianna readied the ship for landing.

Eddie peered out of the open hatch at the inconspicuous landscape. The air was moist and smelled of moss. The grassy meadow that stretched out in front of the Q-Ships disappeared into a rising mist, which obstructed the view. Most disembarking from the Q-Ships were staring up in awe at the bright blue, green, pink and orange lights in the dark sky. They were reminiscent of a phenomenon on Earth that Eddie had watched a program about, the aurora borealis.

"Wow, those are beautiful," Eddie said, still standing inside the ship so he could communicate with Ricky Bobby. The secretive AI had declared in his new executive fashion that there should be no comms once on the planet. He said they'd interfere with the objective of relaxing and unwinding.

"The rainbow lights of Noircun are indeed beautiful," Ricky Bobby stated.

Eddie scratched his chin, deciding how best to say what he was thinking. "I love to see new things, and it's definitely mesmerizing the crew, but I'm not sure how this is worthy of our time."

"Although the lights are worth the trip, and many come from all over to see them," Ricky Bobby began, "they are not the main reason I've brought you all here."

"Oh, really?"

Eddie was relieved. He wasn't sure what he was expecting, but he was hoping it was enough to quell Julianna's anger at the AI. He needed her focused on the current mission, but she was still seething, distracted.

"Will you please lead the crew? I have a series of directions for you," Ricky Bobby requested cryptically.

Julianna stood next to Hatch outside the Q-Ship, mirroring his reluctant stance with her arms crossed in front of her chest.

"Watch your step," Eddie warned, waving Julianna forward. She cast a tentative glance at Hatch before setting off behind Eddie. The rest of the crew slowly joined them, creating a line that streaked across the open area in front of the row of Q-Ships.

Julianna realized the reason for Eddie's caution after a few steps. The slippery grass of the meadow made her feel like she'd lose her footing with each step.

"Where are we going? You said Ricky Bobby gave you instructions?" She looked over her shoulder to see many of the crew struggling with the trek—except for Hatch. He was quite adept at maneuvering over the space, his suctioned tentacles making the trip look easy.

Beside him, Knox lost his balance, slipping and firmly landing on his backside. Julianna frowned slightly before turning her attention back to Eddie.

"Yes, there should be a path leading down in a moment," Eddie told her, pointing ahead at the black mists.

"We're going down, not farther out?" Julianna wondered, picking up on a sound akin to rushing water, except that it reminded her of something else...

I know what the sound is, Pip informed her.

Do tell.

I should wait. I think it's better as a surprise.

When did AIs become obsessed with surprises?

Our limited, confined lives leave us with few thrills.

"If what Ricky Bobby told me was accurate, there isn't much farther out for us to go," Eddie stated.

"Do you have any idea what this is all about?" Julianna asked him.

He shrugged. "I know where we are going, but not what we'll find there."

"Good, I'm glad you're not in on the surprise too," Julianna stated, pulling up beside Eddie. The two were a good bit ahead of the rest now, their enhanced bodies helping them make quick progress.

" 'Too'? Do you mean that Pip is in on this as well?" Eddie asked.

Julianna nodded. "Apparently."

"Huh," Eddie said, his eyes dropping with what looked like disappointment.

Julianna halted abruptly, her vision making out the distance a bit better from their new position. "I see what you mean about having to go down."

Eddie paused beside her, bringing his gaze up. "Oh, wow," he said, his tone startled.

They were standing at the top of a waterfall of sorts, and far below, the effervescent waters stretched for as far as they could see, reflecting the bright colors streaking through the sky. The rushing noise had grown steadily louder, but it sounded like falling pine needles, not water.

"Ricky Bobby brought us to a waterfall?" Julianna asked incredulously.

"I guess he thought it would help," Eddie reasoned.

"This is sort of overboard," Julianna stated.

'**Overboard**,' Pip laughed.

Julianna shook her head. "How do we have an AI intervention?" she asked.

"I don't know if we can. I think we're sort of at their mercy," Eddie said.

Oh yeah, you are, Pip agreed gleefully.

Julianna did her best to ignore him, studying the expanse before them.

"There should be a stone staircase over there." Eddie pointed to a slope by the edge of the cliff.

They moved that direction, and once they were a little closer, Julianna found the makeshift staircase that descended down into a cave-like tunnel. The rushing sound echoed inside the stone structure, which held a chill that was enough to make goosebumps rise on the surface of Julianna's skin, but not enough to make her shiver.

"How did Ricky Bobby even find this?" Eddie asked, his voice muffled by the sound of the falls.

"I'm sure his research brought him to Noircun," Julianna assumed. "He's been all over, finding strange places to study and record."

"That's a helpful AI to have around," Eddie stated with pride.

Is the captain suggesting I'm unhelpful? Pip asked.

Why don't you ask him yourself?

Nah, I'm good. I don't want to cause an issue.

Since when? Julianna joked.

I think it means I need to take a walkabout or soul journey or whatever it is one takes to find and explore their inner self.

Yes, an existential road trip seems like exactly what you need, Julianna said, sarcasm dripping in her tone.

A strange light spilled from the end of the tunnel as they neared the bottom of the staircase. Julianna trailed behind Eddie, running her fingers over the cold wall; it was slick, but not wet from the waterfall's condensation, as she would have expected.

Eddie halted suddenly, and Julianna bumped into him. He was as sturdy as a brick wall, not budging from her charge.

"Sorry," she offered, stepping away.

Eddie reached down, taking her hand—a gesture that caught her off guard. "Don't be. I'm sorry for stopping so abruptly, but this is incredible. You must see it."

Eddie led Julianna out of the tunnel, and she realized that they'd traveled behind the waterfall, which came down in continuous sheets in front of them. Under closer examination, she saw that the water wasn't water at all. The cascade was made of sparkling granules, like sand, in the same array of colors that streaked through the sky.

Julianna had never seen anything like it. *This is the most beautiful thing in the world.*

23

Planet Noircun, Tangki System

"What is it?" Eddie asked, holding out his hand toward the waterfall, but stopping short of actually touching it.

He realized he was still holding Julianna's hand when she pulled him further along the path that snaked around the back of the waterfall, making room for the rest of the crew spilling out of the tunnel behind them.

"Pip says that they are unique organisms that flow out of the ground here, and pool in the reservoir on the other side before evaporating into the sky," Julianna explained carefully, her eyes off to the side as she relayed this information.

"So that's what creates the brilliant light show," Eddie stated.

"No way!" Julianna exclaimed in surprise, coming to an unexpected halt and awkwardly pulling her hand free.

"What is it?" Eddie asked.

A smile unfolded on her face unlike any he'd ever seen. "You're not going to believe this," she breathed.

He watched as the light from the granules streaked across her face, making a strange pattern. "Go ahead and try me."

Julianna cleared her throat and turned to address the crew, who were regarding the sparkling display of falling granules with awe. "According to Pip, these are known as 'jung-fibres'."

"Unbelievable," Hatch chuckled, who was just behind them.

"What's that?" Knox asked him.

Hatch regarded the sparkling bits with a new fascination. "I've only ever heard of them. They're supposedly particles of awareness."

"Huh?" Eddie grunted.

"They can pick up on the consciousness of beings," Julianna explained.

"So they can read our minds," Eddie interpreted.

"Only if you touch them," Hatch qualified, reaching out a tentacle to make contact with the sheet of falling jung-fibres.

The curtain parted, making a new design, and Hatch's face brightened.

"They read your most prevalent thoughts and then construct it for you," Julianna summated.

"'Construct it'?" Eddie asked, scratching his head.

"They are virtual reality creators," she said, making the crowd around her gasp with disbelief.

"No way," Eddie declared.

Julianna smiled. "That's what I said, remember?"

"You'll want to spread out before stepping through, otherwise your realities will spill over into each other," Hatch warned. "Give yourself three to five feet between you and your neighbor."

"Wait, we're going to go through here?" Penrae asked in her natural snake form. The crew had become accustomed to seeing her slither through the corridors of the ship.

"If you want to experience your virtual reality," Hatch reasoned. "It's perfectly safe. You'll step through to the reservoir on the other side, and it will take on the landscape of whatever you're thinking about. I'd encourage you to think of something positive, like your favorite place."

"If these act like true virtual reality creators, we don't have to go through alone," Chester said. "The host would create the reality, and the visitor would see what they see, right?"

"That's correct," Hatch chirped. "But hell if I want any of you ruining my sandy beach and tidal waves."

Chester extended a hand to Marilla, a romantic smile on his face. "You've always wanted to see Paris, right?"

She nodded, taking his hand with a curious smile.

Eddie watched as each of the crew members focused before stepping through the falling jung-fibres, disappearing on the other side. He could only imagine the realities taking shape for each person. Ricky Bobby had given them all their own individual, perfect vacations. It was better than any trip any of them could have planned.

"Alright, we'd better get to it. See you later, Eddie," Julianna stated. She stepped through the curtain, the granules spilling over her shoulders and head as she disappeared.

Eddie's throat tightened as he thought of the reality *he* most wanted to see. Maybe others were escaping to ancient cities or lush beaches, but for Eddie, there may not ever be another opportunity like this. He realized that what he'd see wouldn't be real, but it would feel real, and that was enough.

He closed his eyes, focusing intently before stepping through to the other side.

Julianna found herself in the thermal waters of Clieand, a planet in the Libra system. The virtual reality the jung-fibres served up was incredibly immersive, right down to the cold, misty air and warm pools that glowed a strange, cerulean blue.

However, to Julianna's surprise, after a few minutes of waving her fingers in the supposedly restorative waters, she grew bored. She retreated back to the cave behind the fall.

She wasn't sure why, but she stepped into the spot where Eddie had been, entering his virtual reality. The cool forest air wrapped around her, and she marveled at the majestic trees, their canopy high in the air, blocking most of the rays from the sun.

A short distance away, she spotted Eddie. Standing before him were two figures, a man and a woman, both older. With his back to her, Eddie bowed his head, and a moment later, the two people disappeared.

Julianna took a step forward, a twig underfoot snapping off a sharp crunching sound. Eddie straightened, but didn't turn to face her. She'd invaded his privacy, and yet she didn't feel any remorse.

"You miss them a lot," she observed, referring to the figures she'd recognized as Eddie's parents.

To Julianna's surprise, Eddie wore no look of offense when he spun to face her. Instead, he appeared amused. "Did the reality of your choosing not pan out?"

Julianna shrugged, looking up at a songbird in a tree. "I guess I don't have much of an imagination."

Eddie took a seat on a large, fallen tree trunk, smiling slightly at the ground. "So you decided to sneak into mine, huh?"

Julianna unapologetically pursed her lips as she nodded. "I understand if you're mad."

"I'm not," he said simply. "Maybe I should be, but...I'm actually happy to have your company here. What's the point of going to our favorite place if we don't have someone to share it with?"

Julianna had to agree. That must have been the reason she'd grown bored of the thermal pools so easily, even though she'd always longed to experience them.

She took a seat on the tree next to Eddie. "Where are we?"

He shook his head. "It's how I picture the Redwood forests on Earth, although I've only ever seen pictures."

Julianna grinned. "Which is why your trees aren't quite

large enough. Even when we're the painters of our reality, we're still restricted by our knowledge."

Eddie closed his eyes, and the trunks of the trees around them grew, like a strange hallucination.

"How's that?" he asked.

"Better," Julianna allowed, although the largest Redwoods were the size of Q-Ships, and these were more like Black Eagles.

After a moment of comfortable silence, he said, "I do miss them, obviously, but that's not why I conjured up this reality," Eddie admitted, referring to the vision of his parents.

"You were apologizing," Julianna stated.

Eddie nodded.

"Did it make you feel better?" Julianna asked.

"Not really," Eddie murmured. He pulled up a long piece of grass and began wrapping it around his finger absentmindedly.

"When the threat hit," Julianna began, referring to the event that had happened more than a decade before, "you couldn't have known that Onyx Station was going to be under so much fire."

"I knew that my mom and dad were in danger," Eddie admitted. "I'd gotten word from my commanding officer that the station was being attacked. I knew my parents were there. Yet I made the call to go to Sari, the planet where the attack had originated, and rescue men I hardly knew."

"And that earned you a great honor," Julianna pressed.

"Most would have run from what was considered certain death."

"Most would have run home to save their parents," Eddie corrected.

"Your parents were trained to fight," Julianna countered.

"It isn't the fact that I chose others over my family that has haunted me all this time," Eddie said quietly.

Julianna didn't say a word, instead waiting patiently for Eddie to continue.

"Right before the attack, I'd had a fight with my parents. My mother, as usual was hounding me to get married. My father always teased me about having children." He laughed unexpectedly, no humor in his voice. "That's what parents do, but I took it personally. They wanted me to have the same joys they had, but I didn't see that at the time."

"Hindsight makes everything clearer." Julianna agreed with a minute nod.

A cold look crossed Eddie's face as he brought his eyes up to meet hers. "Instead of shrugging them off, I attacked them. I was hurt that they worked so much and were always away when I was growing up. Like a child, I told them they'd abandoned me, leaving to the responsibility of others to raise while they went off on missions. Why would I do that to a child? They had each other, but often left me. It was stupid. I was stupid and I totally didn't get it."

"You were also younger then," Julianna reasoned. "We're all fools when we are young."

Eddie nodded, but didn't look convinced. "I was

thoughtless, that's for sure. I should have rescued them that day, but I chose not to…part of me was hoping someone else would do it. I'd convinced myself that they'd be okay, but the truth was I didn't go back because I was too ashamed to face them. To tell them I was sorry. It's silly, but there it is. I'm a coward."

"You did go back to Sari and save others, that shouldn't be discounted," she said.

"Yeah, I know you're right."

"You've been carrying these skeletons around for a long time," she said, her voice uncharacteristically sensitive. "Don't you think it's time you forgive yourself? You made a mistake. You said things you regretted, and you lost your chance to make amends, to save those who truly mattered to you. But should you give up your future because you're so ruled by the past?"

Eddie dropped the piece of grass, letting it float down to the ground. He seemed to think for a moment, and then offered her a tender smile. "Do you know what my parents said just now when I confronted them?"

Julianna shook her head.

"They said that it was all okay."

"And you're the architect of this reality," she reminded him.

"Which means, I'm starting to realize that even though I made mistakes, they're not unforgivable," Eddie said, a new lightness in his voice.

The two sat in silence for a long moment enjoying the peace of the forest. The wind shifted the tree branches, making a gentle chiming noise. Julianna regarded the trees and the heavily padded, leaf-strewn ground. The forest wasn't like any she had ever seen; it was different, but felt familiar, like Eddie. She liked that.

She rose when Eddie did, both seeming to know it was time to return to reality, although the decision hadn't been said aloud.

Eddie paused and faced her. "Julianna, you asked if it made me feel better, apologizing to my parents..."

"Yeah. You said it didn't," she replied.

"It didn't. But confiding in you about this...that's made me feel better. Much better than I've felt in years," he admitted, a thoughtful sincerity in his eyes.

"Then it stands to reason that you should continue to do so."

"As long as you keep sneaking into my reality, I plan to do just that."

Eddie offered her his hand, and the two stepped back through to the other side, where what they saw was real and what they felt was pure.

24

Intelligence Center, *Ricky Bobby*, Tangki System

Liesel drilled another hole into the ceiling, shielding her eyes from the metal dust that sprayed down.

"You should have seen it," Marilla stated, holding the ladder for the engineer.

"It sounds delightful," Liesel said. "Paris was supposedly an epicenter for art and culture."

Chester hunched over his workstation, eyeing the screen with intense focus, trying to ignore the distraction of the construction going on behind him. "It was pretty quiet when we were there, as I intended."

"Why didn't you go to Noircun?" Marilla asked Liesel.

The engineer pointed to the ground where various items were strewn. "Mind handing those to me?"

Marilla passed Liesel a strange device that consisted of a short pole, fabric, hooks and handles.

"Thanks," Liesel said, taking only the support stand from her. "I decided it best to stay behind and install these yoga swings, so they'd be ready for you when you got back."

"I still think you need to have your head checked if you think I'm taking my breaks in that trapeze-thing," Chester stated, giving up on work for the moment and spinning around to face the women directly.

"You should really try it before passing judgement. The swing is great for back and neck discomfort." Liesel installed the beam so that it hung horizontally, suspended a few inches from the ceiling.

Chester tilted his head from side to side, stretching his muscles. "My back and neck are fine."

"They won't be, if you keep slouching over your desk," Marilla reprimanded.

Liesel took the other parts of the yoga swing from Marilla and hung them from the short beam. "The jung-fibres do sound amazing, though. I'm glad you got to experience them. Chester, remember that conversation we were having about how there's a synchronization to life, and that we're all connected?"

"I remember you said you could prove it, and then coordinated a distraction so you didn't have to," Chester joked.

"Ricky Bobby, how do the jung-fibres work?" Liesel asked, standing on her tiptoes to hang the yoga swing on the last hook.

"They read the consciousness of the host and then construct the setting they find," Ricky Bobby stated without missing a beat.

"Why?" Liesel challenged.

"Their purpose is unknown, according to my research," Ricky Bobby said.

"And yet you chose this activity because you thought that it would have the best chance of altering the morale of the ship, isn't that right?" Liesel ventured, testing the security of the swing.

"Experiencing a reality of our choosing is considered a magic of sorts," Ricky Bobby reasoned.

"I'd agree with that," Chester said.

"So you're telling me that the best thing we can do is experience ourselves?" Liesel's eyes stayed pinned on her work, although the question was obviously directed at Chester.

"I'm not sure I see where you're going with this," Chester admitted.

Liesel withdrew a wrench from her overalls and tightened the bolts in the ceiling. "Before, you stated that life was meaningless, and that the uncertainty of it made it so our main purpose was to preserve ourselves for as long as possible, until our inevitable death."

"I stand by that notion," Chester said, starting to realize the trap he'd walked into.

"And you, Ricky Bobby?" Liesel asked, tightening another bolt.

"I reserve the right to change my mind," the AI said, his voice low.

"Because if life is meaningless, the act of experiencing ourselves should matter very little. Actually, if we aren't even connected, it would be impossible for the organisms to read us and create our virtual reality." A beat later, Liesel added, "In theory of course."

"Look, Liesel Diesel. I like video games, and those are simulations, but that doesn't mean there's a purpose to all this," Chester argued.

Marilla shook her head. "But that's exactly what it means. What if the purpose is to experience ourselves? And that's what the jung-fibres do, in essence. The only way they can do that is through connectivity."

"And still they will come to an end, and I will, and you too, sweet Mar. Life is progressing toward a breakdown," Chester stated.

"'Life', as in form, but not in consciousness." Liesel slid the wrench back into her pocket. "I'd venture to say that consciousness is timeless."

"Well, here we go talking about souls and stuff again," Chester joked.

"You can call it what you want," Liesel stated. "But, just for fun...Ricky Bobby, when did the jung-fibres originate?"

There was a moment of silence. "I don't have a date of origin for the jung-fibres."

"And why not?" Liesel asked.

"Because they originated with consciousness, a starting point which can't be determined," Ricky Bobby answered.

"Because before we had the ability to actualize, there was no history," Liesel stated triumphantly.

"The consciousness of our life is, in essence, the purpose," Marilla said, sounding breathless. "To know we exist and to experience ourselves—*that's* the reason for all of this. Making even our eventual end, not a concern, but rather a comma in a never-ending sentence. Consciousness always was and always will be, and transitions us forevermore. As long as there's awareness, there will be no end." Marilla paused, then turned to Chester with a smile. "She's deflated your whole point."

The hacker shook his head as he shrugged his shoulders, admitting defeat.

"I couldn't have put it better myself." Liesel pulled the ferret from her front pocket, where he'd been napping. "Would you please hold Sebastian?"

Marilla took the ferret, showing him extra fondness.

"A mind-blowing philosophical conversation, followed by, 'hold my ferret'," Chester said with a laugh.

"The revelations of life often happen during mundane, day-to-day activities," Ricky Bobby stated.

"So you think this was mind-blowing, eh?" Marilla asked, her brown eyes wide with excitement.

"I thought it was interesting, but I'm not sure if it will change my life," Chester admitted.

Liesel tested the yoga swing one more time, yanking on it. Then she stepped off the ladder, angling her head downward. She wrapped her legs around each of the strands of fabric, securing herself with the handles that hung down, doing a full inversion.

With a red face, she said, "A Zen Proverb says, 'Before enlightenment, chop wood, carry water. After enlightenment, chop wood, carry water.'"

Julianna had been exercising in the workout facility, running on one treadmill, while Harley ran on the other, when Penrae had burst in. The Saverus had spoken so fast that Julianna had to make her repeat herself three times. Her emotional state was causing some strange side effects —namely, she was shifting through different forms, like a wire had been fused wrong.

"I really hope I'm right," Penrae stated as they hurried down the long corridor, headed for the Intelligence Center.

"We'll find out momentarily." Julianna gave Penrae a look of encouragement.

She was finding her current reality a bit strange, with the large snake on one side of her, and her new dog friend on the other.

Pip, will you please have the captain meet us in the Intelligence Center? I think he was planning on resting for a little while, so you'll have to wake him.

How do you know he is napping? Was that what he told you when you slipped out from between the sheets?

Pip, you and I aren't friends anymore. And no. Will you just tell Eddie that we might have a breakthrough?

I would, but I can't seem to reach him.

Julianna halted. *What? Is everything okay?*

Yeah, it's fine. I'm just not trying, is all.

Pip, seriously, this is important.

Then I'm sure that Ricky Bobby will do it for you. He's good like that.

Why won't you interface with Eddie? You wanted to be in his head.

Rick Bob said he'd take care of it. I'm going to ring off. I've got a splitting headache.

Pip! Pip! Julianna called after the AI, but received no reply. When she rounded the corner into the Intelligence Center, she halted, surprised by the sight before her.

Liesel, the battlecruiser's chief engineer, hung suspended by fabric a few feet off the ground, her legs in a butterfly position, and her hands praying in front of her chest.

"It was Shunryu Suzuki who said, 'The world is its own magic,'" Liesel shared, her tone airy.

Julianna cleared her throat, gaining the attention of everyone in the room. "Chester, we need you to do some quick surveillance on Savern. Penrae has just woken from a dream."

The Saverus took a deep breath, still looking rattled. "It's true. I think I saw a vision of the ark on Savern."

Chester, Marilla and Liesel simply stared in awe as the Saverus shifted into the form of an elderly Asian man, then to a little girl with pigtails and then back to her original serpentine body.

"Right, can you give Chester some specifics?" Julianna stated, trying to snap everyone into focus.

Running footsteps stole everyone's attention again as Eddie appeared in the doorway, anticipation on his face. "I just heard from Ricky Bobby. What's the news?"

"Nothing yet," Julianna stated, turning back to face Penrae. "Go on, then."

"In my dream, I saw a place I know from the Saverus' history books," Penrae began, flickering through a few different forms as she spoke. "I'm not sure how I didn't consider it before, or why it randomly occurred to me now, but it absolutely makes sense."

"Do you have anything specific?" Chester asked.

"In the dream, the ark was on Savern, in the north of the western hemisphere. That region is the birthplace of the Saverus, and is considered holy ground."

"Chester, does that give you enough information to start a search?" Julianna asked.

The hacker was already busy typing on his computer, sifting through various records. Marilla had also hurried to her own desk and was hurriedly searching.

If I were Ricky Bobby, I'd be telling you a big, fat 'I told you so, regarding the little getaway, Pip stated.

But you're not, and he doesn't gloat like that.

But still, that little R and R does seem to have had its benefits...aside from you and the captain, if you know what I mean. Hint, hint.

I thought you had a headache?

Of course I didn't. That's only something you say when you want to get out of something. You'll learn that, especially now that you and the cap—

Finish that sentence, and I will have you disconnected from me.

You should know that your threats trigger my abandonment issues.

When were you ever abandoned?

It's previous life stuff.

Julianna rolled her eyes, tuning back in as Penrae explained what she'd seen.

"That area is quite large; it will take the scanner several hours, if not a whole day, to do a thorough sweep," Chester stated.

"Wait, your scan includes the entire country of their birthplace," Marilla stated.

"Riiiight…" Chester drew out the word.

Marilla continued to type frantically. "But if you narrow the prameters to include only historical sites, and confine it by markers I've cross-referenced from Savern's history based on importance, then…"

Chester picked up a transmission that Marilla messaged over, and copied the information into the scan. "It boils the search down to a less than hundred-mile radius," he finished for her.

"Which will take how long to search for something that meets the ark's description?" Eddie asked.

Chester's computer made a *ding* sound.

"Approximately no time at all," the hacker grinned.

He pulled up the location marked in red, and zoomed in, revealing a giant warehouse that almost blended in to the yellow hue of the sand, except that it sparkled, since it was covered entirely in gold.

"I believe we've found our ark," Eddie announced excitedly.

Hatch's Lab, *Ricky Bobby*, Tangki System

"Don't touch that!" Hatch warned.

He waddled around the corner to stop Eddie, who was extending a hand toward a device floating in a small anti-gravity chamber about the size of a shoe box.

Eddie's hand snapped down by his leg, and he skirted his eyes to the side like a child caught doing something wrong. "I was just stretching."

"Right," Hatch said, sounding unconvinced. He reached out and opened the container, plucking out the device, which mostly contained a small, handheld screen.

"Ricky Bobby said you had something we'd need for the mission," Julianna stated.

"He was right, but I can't make the captain a brain before you need to leave," Hatch said, offering Eddie an unsympathetic smile. "Sorry, Scarecrow."

Eddie laughed. "And you call yourself a wizard."

"Mechanic, actually," Hatch corrected and held up the device. "Once you find the client in the ark, you'll use this to lead you to the receiver, which will be where the Saverus plan to relocate Savern."

"And then it's ass-kicking time," Eddie said with a smirk.

"How do we know that the client for the Tangle Thief will be located inside the ark?" Julianna asked.

"Because that's the best spot for it to be when operated," Hatch explained. "The Saverus will be most concerned with the ark—"

"Which is why they've plated the building in gold," Eddie interrupted.

Hatch rolled his eyes. "Yes. This is not a rerun, kid. I swear, whatever you do, don't breed. Well, I don't have to worry about that, now, do I? No one would be stupid enough to partner with you."

"Funny you should say that," Pip interrupted overhead.

Julianna shook her head. "Hatch, you were saying? The ark is the best place for the client?"

Hatch stared up to where Pip's voice had broadcast from, but shook his head. "Yes. The pulse sent out from the Tangle Thief will be strongest at its location, to ensure that it is transported. For instance, the bottom of the planet, which is several thousand miles from the northern hemisphere, might actually not make it in the transport, since the device wasn't designed to move objects as large as planets."

"So the Saverus would put the Tangle Thief in or around the ark," Julianna confirmed.

Hatch tied two tentacles behind his back and nodded. "It would go to reason. Which is why I put a tracker into this instrument." He held up the device. "If you're within range, it will help you find the client."

Julianna took the device from Hatch, turning it over in her hands. "And once we locate the client, we hook it into this, and it gives us the location of the receiver?"

"That's correct, Julie," Hatch confirmed, two of his tentacles searching under a workbench. Finally, they retrieved a chrome box, which he lifted and set on the surface of the table.

"What's that?" Eddie asked.

Hatch gave him a repugnant look. "A box."

"Right," Eddie chirped cheerfully.

"What's it for?" Julianna asked.

"Great question," Hatch replied.

Julianna gave Eddie a commiserate expression, slightly smiling at Hatch's obvious bias toward her.

"Once you locate the client—and I do hope you do that fairly quickly, since I'm not ready to be sucked into oblivion," Hatch urged.

Eddie laughed nervously. "We'll do our best, boss."

"That's very comforting. Once you locate the client, stick it in here." Hatch opened a door on the side of the chrome box to reveal a hollow interior. "This device will render the client ineffective, throwing the best wrench we could hope for into the Saverus' plans."

"You're known for throwing wrenches, aren't you, Hatch?" Eddie said playfully.

Hatch ignored him. "So there you go. I've given you a

way to find the receiver, and a method for stopping the Tangle Thief's usefulness. That's all I can do."

Julianna nodded her head in the direction of the chrome vault sitting on the worktable. Eddie took the cue and retrieved it. "Thank you, Hatch. You've given us everything we need. This is great."

Hatch's cheeks puffed out as he averted his eyes. "I admit that what I've given you is pretty incredible, but it will do you no good if you're not able to locate the client in time."

"Don't worry," Julianna said, her tone thoughtful. "We won't let you down."

Hatch shook his head. "No, I'm not sure I've said things the way I meant to." He opened his mouth, but hesitated for several seconds. "What I meant to say was, everyone is depending on you two. We stand to lose so much if you're not successful. But of all the people who could have been chosen to lead this mission, you are the very best. If Ghost Squadron can't stop the Saverus, it can't be done."

Julianna and Eddie both stared at Hatch in quiet disbelief for several seconds.

"Well, don't just stare at me like a bunch of idiots!" Hatch yelled. "You have a damn mission to go on. And need I remind you, you'll be safe in the ark, so do your damn job and protect the rest of us."

Julianna laughed, holding up the device. "We'll see you soon, Hatch."

"I'll be looking forward to it," he said.

"And get ready for a bumpy ride when we return, ready to end the Saverus' fleet," Eddie added.

Hatch shook his head at him, rolling his eyes again. "Oh, get out of here, already. The moment's long since passed."

En route to Planet Savern, Q-Ship, Tangki System

Heat rose off Savern in waves, blurring the structures and red rocks. The planet was covered in sand and sharp mountain ranges. On the edge of a northern coast, a large warehouse sat at least a mile from any other structure. In these holy lands, only the old buildings still stood, which was why the brand new warehouse stood out...well, that and it was plated in twenty-four-carat gold.

The cloaked Q-Ship landed inside the fenced perimeter of the warehouse, not attracting any attention from the guards. Julianna lifted the Saverus goggles to her eyes and peered at the uniformed security patrolling the perimeter. They had the appearance of ordinary humans, but with the goggles, they were revealed to be shapeshifters, their snake forms similar to Penrae's.

"The Saverus dare to construct a gold building on this holy land, but they're not brave enough to reveal their faces," Eddie said, taking the goggles to see for himself.

"No one knows that we still exist, or that our numbers are as healthy as they are," Penrae reminded him.

"It looks like your chance to jump is in about twenty seconds," Julianna said, having timed the rotation of the guards as they patrolled.

"I'm ready," Penrae assured her, standing and pressing down her white lab coat. She had assumed there would be scientists inside the building, taking care of the native animals and plants.

Her extensive knowledge of how the Saverus operated had been invaluable to plotting Ghost Squadron's strategy. In a strange turn of events, Penrae had become an important member of the team.

Penrae straightened the heart-shaped glasses on her face. She'd taken the form of a young woman with long, red hair and speculative green eyes. "I'll radio you when I'm through security."

Julianna nodded, opening the hatch door. She checked the patrol briefly before giving Penrae the signal.

The Saverus sped out of the ship and toward the main entrance of the warehouse, holding the only thing that would get them into the building.

Penrae's breath rattled in her throat and echoed in her head.

This wasn't her home, but these were her people, and she was returning to them. All she'd ever known were the Saverus. It was time for her to walk amongst them once more. It was time she do her part and help end this battle between the Saverus and everyone else.

Penrae had considered her position carefully, and chose her side as only a shapeshifter could: through deception and lies.

Because Penrae knew how the Saverus operated, she knew how this warehouse worked. From the outside, it looked like a regular research facility run by humans, but the security to get in would include something that only a Saverus could bypass.

The queue to get into the warehouse wasn't long, consisting of only two scientists and a few personnel. The person in front of Penrae moved up to the security clearance, offering his arm to the guard. The guard pressed a wand to the man's arm, where a human's pulse would be located. After a moment, the wand glowed green, meaning that the man was a Saverus, shapeshifted into a human.

He was let through, and Penrae stepped forward, her chin held high.

"Beautiful day, isn't it?" Penrae said to the guard.

He smiled, a bit of a flirtatious glint in his eyes. "Yes, but I hope it warms up. The forecast said it could get into the hundreds."

"Let's hope it's right," she said, extending her arm.

"Well, the forecast is about to change, isn't it?"

"That's right," Penrae said with a fake smile.

The guard looked out over the grounds, holding his hand over his eyes like a visor. "Won't be long now. I think you're one of the last to enter the building. Maybe one or two more, and then security personnel."

"And then we'll be off," Penrae said, her voice vibrating with anxiety.

They were using the Tangle Thief *today*. Soon everyone who was to survive the transport would be crammed inside the building, and it would all be over. *Or it will be just beginning.*

The wand swiped over her wrist, but there was no response. The device should only be testing her chemical makeup to ensure her DNA met that of the Saverus, but she suddenly worried there was new technology in place.

"Hmmm. Doesn't seem to be working. Let's try again," the guard said, taking her arm in his hand and again waving the device over her. He kept his fingers pressed against her skin as they waited for the results.

The light glowed green, and Penrae let out a slow breath of relief.

"There it is. Must have been asleep," the guard said.

"Yeah, it must have," Penrae said, hurrying away, all the while aware that the Saverus's eyes were lingering on her back.

She didn't grant herself a moment to observe the strange space within the warehouse. It reminded her of Area 126, but she'd have time to explore later. There were more pressing matters, presently.

"Headed for the western entrance," she whispered into her comm.

"We're headed that way. We'll be in position and ready," Julianna replied.

Penrae politely smiled at everyone she passed, keeping her chin lifted as she hurried through the corridors. She finally halted at a locked roll-up door by the loading docks. The smaller door next to it bore a sign that said, 'Alarm will sound when opened'. Before joining Ghost Squadron, Penrae would never have considered breaking such a rule.

How things have changed.

She pulled a round, disk-like object from her pocket and stuck it to the security device at the top of the door frame that, if triggered, would sound the alarm. There was no way of telling if the dampener would work. All she had was Hatch's word, and her confidence in the mechanic's devices.

She pressed against the release bar, and the door hesitated briefly before opening wide, allowing bright sunlight to spill into the artificially lit area. Silence greeted Penrae's ears, and she let out a huge breath.

Penrae was a Saverus. Her loyalty should be to her race.

At her core, though, she knew the right thing to do, and had been preparing herself for it. She was here to betray her own, with little remorse.

"The western entrance is open," she whispered over the comm.

Julianna fired up the device Hatch had given them to track the client and, by extension, the receiver. Eddie would be responsible for carrying the bulky, chrome vault, and Julianna was thankful that they were going to be cloaked, so he wouldn't be conspicuous.

The minutes that preceded a mission were always

intense. It was the wait before the storm. The quiet before the nonstop noise. Julianna enjoyed those sacred minutes, using them to calm her mind as the tension rose.

"I'd like to take this time to have a little family meeting," Eddie said, cutting into her thoughts.

She looked up from the device she was studying and offered him an insolent expression. "Now?"

He shrugged. "We're alone and in the Q-Ship, which is the only way I'm going to get a response."

"A response about what?" she asked. "What do you want to know?"

He shook his head. "Not from you. From our favorite AI."

"Ricky Bobby isn't here right now," Pip said overhead.

Julianna understood. "I think Eddie was referring to you."

"Oh, well, flattery will get you nowhere. What do you want?" Pip asked grumpily.

Eddie didn't appear deterred. "Why are you avoiding me?"

"It's not you. It's me," Pip stated. "You're a great guy. One that any AI would be lucky to have. I just don't think I'm ready to give you what you want. Call it immaturity on my part."

Eddie shook his head, chuckling softly. "You're the one who begged to be paired with me. I even gave you access to my body."

"Look, we're both adults here," Pip continued. "And that was consensual."

"You slapped me in the face with my own hand."

Pip laughed. "We did have some good times."

"I totally understand," Eddie said. "You're a one-person kind of AI. No feelings hurt, but I'd at least like it all out in the open."

"I have a secret," Pip said coyly.

Julianna's eyes widened as she stared at Eddie, not sure what to say.

"We can be honest here," Eddie encouraged.

"Fine. I'm in love with Julianna," Pip blurted out.

"No. You're. Not," Julianna said, emphasizing each word.

Pip sighed. "Wow, I feel a lot better. Alright, so now we can just go back to normal."

"Not even close," Julianna said, shaking her head.

Eddie laughed. "If you do in fact have feelings for Jules, it was probably pretty uncomfortable for you to be in my head, huh?"

Julianna pressed her eyes shut, wondering how her life had gotten so completely strange. *Is it too late to sign up for a normal life? One that doesn't include an obsessive AI and impossible missions to save the galaxy...*

"I'm not going to lie," Pip replied. "Being in the captain's head wasn't the pancake feast I figured it would be. But at least we tried it."

"No hard feelings," Eddie said with a laugh. "We'll have Hatch disconnect you when we return."

"I do lament losing access to a body, but I feel this is for the best," Pip related.

"Well, I'm glad you two feel better, because I'm completely mortified," Julianna stated, opening her eyes—

although looking at Eddie made her flush with embarrassment.

"One day, you'll be able to confess your true feelings, and when that time comes, I'll be here," Pip said, his tone cheerful.

"Headed for western entrance," Penrae whispered over the comm.

Perfect timing. Julianna exhaled, activating her cloaking belt. "We're headed that way. We'll be in position and ready."

Saverus Ark, Planet Savern, Tangki System

Eddie's body flickered a few times as he entered the warehouse, and then became completely solid.

"Uh-oh," he said, peering down.

"Fuck, the cloak must not work in here because of the gold plating," Julianna figured, her image solid as well.

"We're not exactly in disguise," Eddie said, putting the cube-vault awkwardly under one arm.

"No, we're not, which means we're going to attract a shitload of attention." Julianna looked around, like she was searching for a costume.

Eddie pushed the box into Penrae's hands, catching her by surprise. "You're in charge of this." He pulled his gun out of its holster, feeling marginally better. "I'll be in charge of this."

Julianna nodded somewhat reluctantly.

"Penrae, you do whatever it takes to keep your cover," Eddie ordered. "Keep some distance from us, in case we get caught. You might be able to swoop in and save us, or at least provide a distraction."

"Okay." She looked like she'd just swallowed a large rock.

Julianna held up the tracking device, trying to get a signal, and pointed it toward a dark corridor. "Good news. The client appears to be in here."

"Any chances it's close by?" Eddie asked hopefully.

"If by 'close', you mean 'clear on the other side of this supposed ark', then yes," Julianna replied.

"Rats, why can't they make it easy for us?" Eddie complained.

"You wouldn't like easy," Julianna pointed out.

"True," he agreed.

"We're headed this way," Julianna said to Penrae, pointing at the long corridor. "It looks like that hallway loops back around." She pointed at the one behind them.

"I'll go that way and meet up with you," Penrae said. "I'm on the comm, if anything goes wrong."

Julianna and Eddie nodded before striding off in the opposite direction.

Penrae felt like there was a huge sign on her head that said, *'Traitor'*. Each time she passed someone it became increasingly difficult to look them in the eyes. It was only a matter of time before someone questioned her on what she was doing and asked why she wasn't in her designated place.

When a group of Saverus dressed in lab coats rounded the corner, Penrae ducked into the nearest room.

She squinted from the bright, overhead lights, feeling like she'd just walked into one of the sun rooms that her kind had on all their ships. They mimicked the sunlight on Savern, which Saverus needed regular exposure to for their overall well-being. She hadn't worked up the nerve to tell the captain and commander that it was something she'd require on *Ricky Bobby*. Maybe when she proved her usefulness with this mission.

As her eyes adjusted, Penrae realized that there were tropical plants filling the large room. They'd been planted in rock beds, and filled the air with a freshness that she relished. She touched the blossom of a hibiscus flower, enjoying its softness. It had been a while since she had been in the wild, and something about these plants seemed to call to a part of her that was deeply buried.

Maybe her ancestors weren't wrong to want to preserve Savern as it used to be, but their way of going about it was truly horrendous. She reminded herself that the Elders had been run off Savern because they were cruel to their own. Her race suffered by their own hand.

Penrae smiled as a butterfly landed on a succulent plant. The room was peaceful, with its quiet plants and bright, artificial light.

Something whizzed by Penrae's head, and her hair whipped back. She spun around, looking for the source of the speed. Hovering in the air, flapping its wings in a blur, was something Penrae had read about but hoped never to meet.

The eyes of the vampiric hummingbird flashed red, a hungry vengeance in its stare.

Penrae backed up, but that only set the bird off. It dove at her, beak first. Penrae covered her head with her free hand, stumbling backwards on a cactus and dropping the cube. The quills pierced her skin, and she shrieked in pain.

The hummingbird hovered over her body. Its head whipped to the side, its eyes landing on her bleeding leg.

"No," Penrae cried, scrambling backwards.

The bird dove again, this time piercing her skin with its beak. She slapped at the bird, connecting with its beating wings, but it defended itself against her attacks. Penrae kicked her leg into the air, trying to throw off the creature who was buzzing around it with gross excitement.

Grabbing the bloodthirsty hummingbird with both hands, Penrae yanked it off her leg and threw it across the room, where it landed with a *thump*. Not caring that she might have just killed one of the last remaining vampiric hummingbirds in existence, she grabbed the vault and sprinted for the door, desperate to get as far from that room as she could.

"Should we check on Penrae?" Julianna asked, peeking around a corner to look for witnesses.

"I'm sure she's fine," Eddie said, his eyes on the hallway they'd just come from. "She's probably buzzing around this place without a problem, since she blends in so well."

Julianna nodded, looking at the device. "The good news

is that the client appears to be in a room on the other side of the next corridor."

"What's the bad news?" Eddie asked, preparing himself.

"The room is fucking gigantic."

"Like the size of an ark?" Eddie joked.

Jules rolled her eyes. "If we can stay out of sight until we get to the client, we're in good shape. I'm okay with shooting our way out of here, but I'd feel better doing that with a piece of the Tangle Thief in tow."

"Agreed." Eddie slipped around Julianna, taking the lead. She gave him a cold stare that communicated her disapproval. "You can go first *after* we get the client," he told her defensively.

She held her finger to her mouth, straightening, indicating she'd heard something.

Eddie heard it too. It was coming from behind them. He opened the door closest to them and encouraged Julianna to follow. It slipped shut behind them just as two figures strolled around the corner. Eddie was able to observe them through a small window of mirrored glass in the side panel. The figures halted in the middle of the hallway, seeming to review a stack of files together.

"They'll move on," Eddie told Julianna, reading her look of worry.

He turned around, taking in the dim room they'd entered. Shelves with various-shaped cubbyholes lined the wall. From their distance, Eddie could only make out pairs of reflective eyes staring back at him from a few of the cubbies.

"What do you suppose those are?" he asked, taking a step closer.

"Eddie…" Julianna said, a warning in her voice.

"What are you worried about? Whatever is in those holes isn't big enough to do us any harm."

"I think we should leave whatever it is alone," she argued. "Those scientists will be gone soon."

"Yes, but in the meantime, I'm just going to have a quick look-see."

Eddie ducked down, peering into one of the holes. Large, round eyes stared back at him. As he got closer, he could make out a pointed face, covered in short, soft fur. A small creature was perched close to the edge of the shelf, its pink nose wiggling.

"Well, hello there, little buddy," Eddie said to the creature.

It looked like a cross between a koala bear and a kitten. The animal blinked up at him in curiosity.

"Eddie, I don't like this."

"You're the animal lover," he teased, extending a hand to the creature. "Need I remind you that you once risked your life, and our mission, to save a bunch of rabbits on Kai?"

"You shouldn't remind me, if you want to live much longer," Julianna said, her tone impatient. "Come on, those scientists are continuing down the hallway. Let's get ready to go."

"She's really a nice lady and would probably take you home with her," Eddie told the animal in a baby voice. It tilted its head to the side, its nose sniffing wildly, taking in

Eddie's scent. "I think it likes me," Eddie said, smiling over his shoulder at Julianna.

A sharp pain stabbed through his fingers. He whipped around to find the animal clamped onto his hand, where blood was squirting out. Eddie held back a scream and waved his hand through the air, trying to throw off the strange, murderous creature.

"I told you," Julianna said in a hush, running over and stopping at his side.

"It won't let go," he said, holding his hand still. The furry creature had its mouth around three of his fingers and part of his palm, its eyes roving back and forth like looking for its next point of attack.

Julianna pulled out her gun.

"Are you crazy?" Eddie nearly yelled. "You can't shoot this thing."

"Why not?" she asked, completely serious.

"Because it's…well, it's a furry critter."

Julianna's eyes darted to the side. She slid her arm in front of Eddie's chest, encouraging him back. He turned to find a dozen pairs of eyes blinking back at them from the cubbies.

"I'm guessing that all of those guys are as hungry as this one," Julianna stated.

Eddie lifted his hand, where the creature still dangled. The animal didn't look to be growing weary, but blood was dripping from Eddie's hand onto its fur.

"Any ideas?" he wanted to know.

"Besides blowing its brains out?" Julianna asked.

"Yeah, besides that."

Julianna looked at the window and then to the dark cubbies where the animal had been perched. "What do you want to bet that these little fuckers normally live underground?"

Eddie looked up at the ceiling, which was lined with dim lights. "Yeah, that makes sense to me."

"Let's take it for a ride and try to find a bright light." Julianna suggested.

Eddie shook his hand, hoping the thing would let go. When it didn't he said, "Okay, but this thing hurts like a bitch."

"Well, maybe next time, you'll listen to me when I tell you to not touch the native animals."

"Yeah…'next time'," he said, following her out the door and into the empty hallway.

Penrae was still running when she rounded a corner, nearly colliding with a man in a smart, black suit. He reached out and grabbed her arm to keep her from falling back, and his gray eyes slid over her. The box nearly fell from her grasp.

"Are you all right?" he asked.

"I'm fine." Trembling, Penrae pulled out of his grasp and took several steps backward, leaving a trail of blood from her shoe.

"You're bleeding," the man said, closing the distance quickly.

"I-I-I fell," she stuttered.

"And why were you running?" the man asked.

"I'm late," she lied, hurrying around the man.

He sniffed loudly. "That smell...I recognize it."

Penrae whipped around. "I was working in the tropical desert when I fell on a cactus. That's what you smell."

The man sniffed again, this time more fervently. "No, this isn't a plant smell. *Your* smell...it reminds me of someone."

Penrae's eyes widened. *No. He couldn't be.* She nearly stumbled as she backed away, frantically reviewing her options. The man reached out for her, but she made space between them. He snatched her anyway.

His gray eyes narrowed, and his lips pinched together. "Penrae, is that you? Have you come home for your punishment?" Verdok asked, his tone sharp.

A hot pain shot down Penrae's spine, and she spun around, doing the only thing she knew. She fled.

Julianna had been right. The bright light in the hallway instantly made the deceptive furry animal release its death grip on Eddie's hand, and it scurried off in the opposite direction.

"I think someone might notice a bloody animal on the loose," Eddie said, wrapping his wounded hand in a piece of cloth he'd pulled from his shirt.

"Then we'd better hurry," Julianna stated, pointing at a door at the far end. "The client is through there."

Eddie pulled his gun from its holster. "I sort of doubt that it won't be heavily guarded at this point."

"Then we'd better be ready to deactivate it and run like hell," Julianna said, pressing her comm. "Penrae, do you copy?"

Silence.

"Penrae?" Julianna tried again.

When there was no answer, she strode for the far side of the hallway.

"What's the plan?" Eddie asked, scanning the space at their backs.

"Get the client and get the fuck out of here."

"Have I told you lately how much I appreciate how uncomplicated you are?" Eddie asked, a laugh in his voice.

"Tell me later," Julianna said, raising her gun. "We've got company."

Two guards strode around the corner, at first not seeing Julianna and Eddie. Jules fired twice, knocking them out swiftly. They fell to the ground, almost instantly morphing into their snake forms.

"So you're not sharing, are you?" Eddie teased, picking up the pace and running on his toes beside Julianna.

"The next ones are all yours," she promised, sliding around the corner to check the next hallway, as he did the same on the other side of her.

When they'd checked that all was clear, they slid back the door to the large room where the Tangle Thief was located.

It was the size of the landing bay on *Ricky Bobby*, but was crammed with crates and clear cases. The room was incredibly orderly, with the rows stacked at an even, middling height so that they could see to the far side. In the center sat a single case, and suspended in the middle of it was the client.

Eddie started forward, but Julianna stopped him. He gave her a curious look.

Silently, she pointed to the device in her hands. It showed that the client wasn't straight ahead of them, as it appeared to be, but rather in the far corner of the room.

Eddie smiled. It was a decoy. The Saverus had either been expecting them, or the fake had been there for a while, serving as bait for anyone who would try to stop the plan.

Julianna nodded to the right, indicating the closest route to the client, and the two set off soundlessly.

Penrae ran, not daring to look behind her. She had no idea how she'd escape Verdok.

Of course he found me. I was foolish not to consider that he'd be here. His vengeance will be overwhelming when he catches me. If he catches me...

Penrae knew it was dangerous, but she whipped her head over her shoulder to check her progress, and nearly stumbled from the shock. Verdok was so close. He slithered rapidly behind her, having shifted into snake form.

Since she was carrying the box, her movement was limited. Still, none of it would matter if she didn't survive to get it back to Julianna and Eddie. She slipped into the form of Sebastian the ferret, and the chrome box clattered to the ground. Small and agile, she scurried up a vent shaft that ran along the wall and ceiling, moving the way she'd often seen the ferret do. When at the top of the shaft, Penrae slipped through the slats of the ventilation system.

Verdok hissed, his shadow swaying back and forth. "Don't forget that wherever you hide, I'll be able to sniff you out." He disappeared.

Penrae wasted no time, speedily climbing through into a nearby room. It was lined with shelves that were filled with jars. Running along the crammed shelves, Penrae's ferret eyes made out seed-like objects in the jars.

The door to the room creaked as it opened.

"Penrae, I smell you," Verdok sang, glee in his voice.

Dammit! I couldn't have fallen into a room with a hungry, serpent-eating dragon? Seeds are useless!

She scurried between the jars, making a few teeter. She worried she was leading Verdok straight to her. *And I'm a damn ferret, something he can gobble up in an instant!*

But Penrae didn't know what else to do. She'd been intimidated by Verdok since she could remember. He'd always bossed her around. Made her take the blame. Bullied her.

And in the end, he'd murder her.

She backed up, watching his swaying shadow near from the far side of the aisle.

"You know, Penrae," Verdok began with a hiss. "I knew you'd return. I knew, when Savern was about to disappear, that you'd want to be a part of our great planet."

Penrae nearly slipped off the other side of the shelf,

having backed up blindly. The sound of Verdok's voice made her insides vibrate with fear. It always had.

"The thing is, I can't have you joining us on the new planet," Verdok hissed. "You mess up everything; I can only imagine how you'd screw up the new Savern. Not to mention the lies you'd tell about me."

Penrae carefully climbed up the side of the shelf, making her way to the next level. She had a plan, but she wasn't sure it was a very good one. Actually, she was mostly unsure of whether she could pull it off, but she had nothing to lose at this point.

"Do you remember when we were younger, how you told the Elders it was me who made the mistake on the mission?" Verdok asked, disapproval heavy in his tone.

*It **was** you,* Penrae thought bitterly.

"And then later, when we were assigned this mission, you tried to get me to accept your plan." Verdok laughed. "You tried to get me to let the old doctor go, thinking he'd lead us to a clue. You were so shortsighted; you are even more so now."

Verdok slithered around the corner. He was directly below Penrae's shelf.

"Come out of hiding and take your punishment like a good girl. Your time has come."

I'll come out, alright, Penrae thought, and she took off running, knocking against each of the jars as she went, sending them tumbling over the side of the shelf to rain glass down on Verdok's head.

He shrieked his disappointment, slithering quickly to avoid the falling objects, but still staying in the line of fire.

Taking a deep breath, Penrae leapt off the end of the shelf, morphing into a figure who she looked up to, a human she wanted to be just like.

Verdok halted. Glass shards punctured his scales in many places, and his eyes fumed with anger.

In the form of Julianna, Penrae held up her gun and pointed it directly at Verdok. Before he could react, she released the safety, as she had seen the commander do a number of times.

"It's your turn to be punished," Penrae growled, then she pulled the trigger with zero hesitation.

According to the tracker, the client was only a short distance ahead. There were a few crates, but Julianna went for the closest one, pulling off the lid, making more noise than she should.

"It's not here," she said, moving on to another crate.

Eddie nodded, his eyes scanning. Footsteps clapped on the concrete, making Julianna tense.

"Keep going," Eddie encouraged. "I'm going to go cut these guys off."

Julianna looked up to argue, but catching the serious look in Eddie's eyes, she nodded instead. She dove back into her search, with only two more crates to go.

Eddie sprinted in the direction of the sound of the footsteps. Five guards stopped in the center of the large room as soon as they spotted him.

He halted too, taking in his surroundings. When he noticed a side door, he turned to face the guards. "Hey, guys. How's it going? I was looking for the little snakes' room. Can you help me out?"

They lifted the weapons they held, not looking as comfortable holding them as seasoned soldiers would. But there were still five of them and one of him.

"So, no to directions?" Eddie joked, and he darted behind the closest shelf as the gunfire started.

Not only were they horrible shots, but Eddie was incredibly fast. He was at the door before they even realized he was no longer hiding behind the crates. He whipped it open, intent on drawing the imposters as far from Julianna as possible so she could find the client.

He slowed when he arrived in the next room. It was more of a greenhouse than a storage room, like the one he'd just exited. Rows and rows of plants that resembled ferns lined the short room. A quick glance around told Eddie that he'd picked the wrong place to hide; it was a dead end. He spun back to the door he'd come through.

I'll just have to pick these guys off one at a time.

From the corner of his eyes, he noticed the plants start to sway slightly. Thinking it was a hallucination, he chanced a glance. The leaves of the plants were indeed unfurling; a stem reached up from each center, with a bud at the top.

Curious, Eddie watched as all the buds blossomed on

the different plants. It was mesmerizing, but he was trying to keep one eye on the door.

And then music emanated from the plants—a soft, melodic tune that instantly put him at ease.

His eyelids nearly slipped shut, and he was shocked at how quickly these plants' effects worked. He took a step forward and stumbled, feeling drunk for the first time since being enhanced.

It was precisely at that moment that he realized that he couldn't fight the sleep-inducing effects of the plants. He was powerless against them.

His legs gave out, sending him flat to the floor. He tried one last time to fight the urge to sleep, but decided it would be best to shut his eyes for a moment while he got his strength. He took a deep breath, satisfied with this plan, and fell into a deep, dreamless sleep.

Penrae's hand shook as she stared at the dead body before her.

Verdok's.

I did it. I finally faced my demons! Rather, Julianna did... Does my form matter, as long as it was my hand that slayed the beast that haunted me my whole life?

Penrae shifted back into the form she'd taken when she entered the warehouse, but didn't move from her spot.

"I've got the client," Julianna's voice echoed over the comm.

Penrae stayed frozen, continuing to stare at Verdok's dead body.

"Penrae? Are you there?" Julianna asked.

"Y-Y-Yes, I'm here," Penrae stuttered, backing up for the door.

"Do you have the vault?" Julianna asked. "We need to get out of here."

Penrae looked down at her empty hands. The vault was in the corridor where she'd dropped it.

"I can get it to you," she said, not wanting to let Julianna down.

"Hurry. I'm in the main room."

The guards stood outside the door the trespasser had disappeared through.

Mon shook his head at the other men. "That human had no idea where was he was headed," he said, handing the others headphones from where they were stored beside the room.

"Think he's sound asleep by now?" one of the other guards asked.

"Probably, but let's give it another minute," Mon said with a laugh.

They'd normally just bust in there and capture the trespasser, but, unluckily for this guy, they'd been given orders to quickly eliminate anyone interfering with the day's mission.

Julianna let out a huge sigh when Penrae hurried over, carrying the vault. Her face was pale, and one pant leg was covered in blood, but otherwise, she looked unharmed.

The door to the vault stuck slightly when she tried to open it, but it came open with a bit more effort. Julianna dropped the client into the vault and was flooded by a huge wave of relief.

She pressed her hand to her comm. "Black Beard, we've secured the client. We're ready to go."

There was no answer.

I've downloaded the location of the receiver from the tracker, Pip informed her.

Oh, good. That was fast.

Well, I'm pretty talented.

Send over the coordinates to Ricky Bobby and inform them we'll be back soon. She reached out to Eddie again over the comm. "Black Beard, do you copy?"

Once more, the comm remained silent. Penrae gave Julianna a cautious stare.

Pip, will you check on the captain? Julianna asked him. *It's important,* she added a moment later.

Yes, of course, he answered.

Julianna directed Penrae to the exit, and they snaked their way to a less traveled corridor, where the lights were dimmer. They needed to get out of the building and to the Q-Ship.

The captain appears to be passed out, Pip stated.

Julianna halted. *What? How?*

His vitals show he's fine, but sleeping, Pip said. **In a patch of plants,** he added a beat later.

Those can't be normal plants.

I suspect you're right.

Piiiip, Julianna said, drawing out his name.

Yes, Jules? he asked innocently.

Pip, she bit on the word now.

Yes, yes, fine, fine. I'll go and save the day.

Mon eyed the door handle. He didn't have much combat training, which was why he was glad the invader had run straight for the comatose-fern room. "Alright, take this guy down to the holding cell, and we'll deal with him there. No blood on the plants."

The others nodded before clapping their headphones over their ears.

The world went silent as Mon opened the door.

Something charged through it, bowling Mon over. He was shoved back into a large case, the air knocked out of him.

The man who should have been asleep threw a foot across one of the guard's faces, knocking him to the ground. When two more guards raced for him, the intruder reached out, grabbing them by the chin with either hand, and sent them flying several yards. Like he had eyes in the back of his head, the trespasser then reached for his gun at his waist and spun around to the guard charging at him. He shot once, killing his would-be attacker dead.

Mon hadn't dared to move, only stared paralyzed at the man who appeared almost robotic in his actions.

The trespasser pivoted and faced Mon, a mechanical sort of smile on his face. "See you later," the man said, firing at him.

Saverus Ark, Planet Savern, Tangki System

Where is he? Julianna ordered.

He's on his way, Pip answered, sounding bored.

Julianna started the preflight checks, her mind buzzing with adrenaline.

There are two more guards at the exit. Hold up while I show them how I tap dance.

Pip, just get out of there.

'Tap dance' is another way of saying 'kick some ass'.

Julianna let out a heavy breath. She initiated a connection with Ricky Bobby.

"Strong Arm here. Do you have the coordinates for the Saverus fleet?"

"Yes, Strong Arm," Jack's voice came over the comm. "We're waiting for your arrival."

"The Saverus have to be onto us at this point," Julianna murmured.

"I fear you're right."

"I think you better head off without us."

"Okay, I think that's a smart move. We're set to gate," Jack responded.

"The Saverus fleet is huge and well stocked," Julianna said, tapping her fingers on the controls.

"And they'll shift to look just like us, but we're prepared," Jack said.

"And the flyers?" Julianna asked. She should be onboard Ricky Bobby when they attacked the fleet.

"Everything is in position," Jack assured her.

"Okay, we'll meet you there," Julianna stated, inputting the coordinates so they could gate after leaving Savern's atmosphere.

How much do you like the captain's face? Would you like it with a few more scars? Pip asked.

Don't play games with me, Julianna warned.

I'm only kidding. He's pretty much unharmed, except for a kick to the groin, but it couldn't be avoided.

The hatch door opened, and, like a robot, Eddie strode into the ship.

Soldiers ran after him, their weapons pointed. Julianna wanted to race to Eddie, but instead she remembered her training and lifted the Q-Ship into the air, avoiding the spray of bullets from the ground forces. She flew the ship swiftly up into the heavens, where a battle she needed to be a part of was soon beginning.

Unclassified System, Saverus Fleet

Ricky Bobby cloaked as soon as it reached the coordinates for the Saverus fleet. A large battlecruiser hovered in the center, surrounded by a dozen ships of various sizes.

This pocket of space was where they'd planned to relocate Savern, not even caring that they'd be destroying an entire galaxy.

"Ready the mains," Fletcher stated, his eyes intently on the radar.

"Weapons are ready," Ricky Bobby said overhead.

"Fire on the main ship on my command," Fletcher said, knowing they only had one chance before the Saverus realized they were there and started their own attack.

"Three, two, one, fire," Fletcher commanded.

Three explosions spread across the Saverus ship.

"Their shields are holding," Ricky Bobby stated. "They've deployed single fliers."

"Deploy Black Eagles," Fletcher ordered.

The line of Black Eagles streaked through the air, firing at the Saverus's ships. It didn't take long for the enemy fleet to take on the appearance of the Black Eagles.

"Use your radar, pilots," Fletcher stated. "Pretend you're flying blind, and prepare for another attack."

He exhaled, running his hand over his forehead. He knew that Ricky Bobby was more prepared for this attack than the first, but he wasn't sure if this was a battle they could win.

The Saverus's fleet is just too damn big.

Eddie shook his head, slow to wake.

"How do you feel?" Julianna said, preparing to jump the ship.

"Like I've been asleep for a year." Eddie stared around disoriented. "How did I get out of there?"

"You can thank Pip for that," Julianna said.

"Forget about it," Pip stated dully.

"Are you prepared to be on guns?" Julianna asked.

Eddie straightened, nodding. "Yeah, I'm good to go."

"Great, because I have a feeling this is going to be a fast and brutal fight."

"We're taking a lot of hits," Lars yelled over the comm.

Fletcher had wondered if the Kezzin was up for flying so soon after being injured, but telling him 'no' didn't seem like an option.

"There are too many of them," Escrema stated, her voice breathless.

Fletcher could see the pilot was right. There were at least four times as many enemy fliers on the radar as they had.

"The main ship's shields are holding at fifty percent," Ricky Bobby reported.

The only advantage that they had was that their own battlecruiser was still cloaked, but it would soon be visible on radar, and then Ricky Bobby would be taking hits from all sides.

A Q-Ship sped dangerously close to the bow of the ship.

"Hey, there, Ricky Bobby," Julianna's voice said over the comm. "How's it going?"

"Glad you could make it," Fletcher said, his voice heavy.

"Give us the big picture," Eddie said.

"Our fliers are taking a serious hit, and our weapons are quickly depleting. I'm not sure we can do much more damage to their main ship," Fletcher said, hating the defeated tone of his voice.

"Has communication with the fleet been established?" Julianna asked.

"I've got a link ready," Ricky Bobby told her.

"We need to make them surrender," Eddie stated.

"How can we do that, when we're unprepared to win this fight?" Fletcher wanted to know.

"They've located our position. Prepare to take hits," Ricky Bobby warned.

"Fuck." Fletcher gripped the side of the strategy table.

"Hey!" Hatch yelled, waddling onto the deck. "I might have a solution."

"Go on, Hatch," Julianna urged.

Hatch's eyes lingered on Fletcher before looking to the radar. "You have the client from the Tangle Thief in the vault, correct?"

"That's correct," Eddie answered.

"I'm guessing that the receiver is in the battlecruiser," Hatch stated.

"Right, and you said if the Saverus were successful, that the Tangle Thief would make room for the planet, keeping their fleet safe," Julianna said.

"That's correct," Hatch chirped. "But—and I'm not completely sure about this—but if the client is dropped onto the same location as the receiver and then gets acti-vated, the two should cancel each other out."

"Meaning that there would be no transport?" Eddie asked.

"Correct," Hatch said.

"But, then, what would happen?" Julianna asked.

"A giant goddamn explosion," Hatch answered.

"So you're telling us that if we…" Julianna trailed off.

"That's right, Julie," Hatch confirmed. "I can tell you how to recalculate the client."

"It would blow up their entire fleet, though," Eddie reasoned.

"Not before giving us all time to get away," Hatch said, his voice boiling with excitement.

"But it would blow up their entire fleet," Julianna repeated.

"Your point?"

Julianna sighed. "Give us a minute."

After a brief discussion, Eddie flipped back on the comm. "Ricky Bobby, patch us in to the Saverus."

"You're connected," Ricky Bobby said.

"Saverus, this is Ghost Squadron," Julianna's voice rang out clear and loud. "We've stopped your plan to take Savern. We have your ships surrounded, and the means to annihilate you. You have two options: stay and continue to fight us, or retreat and live peacefully amongst us. We don't want to see this turn into an extinction." Julianna stared back at Penrae, who gave her a nervous smile.

The line remained quiet for a long moment.

"We haven't been stopped, only delayed," a voice said with a hiss over the comm.

"Saverus, if you stay on your current path, you will be destroyed," Julianna warned. "I encourage those of you who don't want this to end badly to leave."

"Our own will not desert the Elders," the voice said.

However, many of the medium-sized ships began moving out of formation and putting distance between themselves and the main ship.

Julianna looked up at Eddie with surprise. "They might have sense like Penrae, after all." She continued her message. "Elders, we're giving you one last warning. If you continue to fight, you will be destroyed."

"You don't have the means to do that," the thin voice taunted on the other end of the line.

Julianna severed the connection and shook her head. "I really fucking hate being underestimated." She gave Eddie a knowing look, and he nodded.

"Fletcher, gather our ships and prepare to gate," he ordered. "The rest is up to us."

"Copy that, Black Beard," Fletcher replied. "I'm bringing the Black Eagles home."

Julianna had set the calculations on the client exactly as Hatch had instructed her. It was crazy to realize that this small device could have such an incredible impact. It just proved again that small things should not be underestimated.

The client had been loaded into the drop shaft that Hatch had installed without knowing if it would ever have a use.

"Can you get a little closer?" Eddie asked, operating the release for the drop.

"You know I can," Julianna smirked, steering the Q-Ship over the surface of the Saverus battlecruiser. Being this close was risky, but they wouldn't be there for long, and by the time the radar picked up their presence, they'd be gone.

"Initiating drop in three, two, one," Eddie said and pressed the button.

From the bottom of the Q-Ship, railgun technology shot the client, landing it on top of the battlecruiser. It clung to its surface, magnetized to the ship.

Julianna pulled the Q-Ship up and activated the thrusters, speeding as far away as she could in the ten seconds that followed. The only ship that remained in the open space was the large battlecruiser. She activated the jump, sending the Q-Ship on a path back to Ricky Bobby.

She knew what would happen to the battlecruiser, and she was glad she wouldn't have to see it get blown to bits.

Loading Dock, *Ricky Bobby*, Tangki System

Julianna picked up the ball that Harley dropped at her feet, and waved it in front of his face, taunting him. "Do you want this?" she teased.

He watched the ball intently, his tongue hanging out one side of his mouth, and a smile in his eyes. She was grateful that even after the upgrade, he hadn't lost his free nature.

Of course I want it, Harley said.

She threw the ball, sending it to the other side of the loading dock, and Harley took off speeding after it.

Eddie smiled at her as he approached, his hands pressed into his pockets, and a coy look on his face.

"What?" she said, a growl in her voice.

"Nothing," he sang.

"I don't want to hear it."

"Which part? The part about how I knew you'd warm

to the dog, or that you look cute throwing a ball?" he asked playfully.

She whipped around, mock anger on her face. "Teach, don't mess with me."

He waved his hand, pretending he'd been burned. "Back to last names, are we? Come on, Freggin, you know I'm only playing with you."

She smiled, not able to even pretend to be mad. *'Teach'*. It sounded so strange calling him that now. It felt like it had been a lifetime since she'd first met the idiot before her.

That's what she used to think he was, but over time, layers had been revealed. Eddie was anything but an idiot.

"How's Pip, after the whole procedure?" Eddie asked.

Tell him that I'm fine, but I hear that having an AI removed could have lasting effects on one's manhood, Pip said.

Julianna rolled her eyes. *I'm not saying that.*

"He seems to have recovered just fine, although I probably won't hear the end of him wanting another body," Julianna stated.

My *own* body, Pip said. **Next time, I want my *own* body.**

How do you know there will be a next time?

Do you want to talk about my little confession? Pip asked, ignoring her question.

I was thinking of erasing that from my mind, to tell you the truth.

Hatch is working on that technology, Pip said casually.

You're not really in love with me.

No, but I'm protective, all the same. And I didn't like being in the captain's head. Sue me for biting off more than I could chew.

We've all had desires that later we reconsidered.

You see, that's what I love about you. You're so levelheaded.

Would you stop using that word?

Which one? 'Love'? I think what you mean to ask is will I teach you how to say it.

That's not what I mean.

Eddie had picked up the ball that Harley retrieved, and thrown it again. He gave Julianna a sideways glance before offering her another smile.

"What?" she demanded, sensing he was holding something back.

"I was just thinking, maybe we could take a little getaway."

"A getaway?" she questioned. "Are you serious? We just crossed three systems yesterday."

"I meant more of a vacation," Eddie said, looking shy for maybe the first time ever.

"A vacation?" she asked.

"Yeah, it's this thing that people do when they want to take a break from working," Eddie said with a laugh.

"I know damn well what a vacation is. I just never felt much like taking one before."

"Well, maybe things are a little different now," Eddie said, holding out his hand to her.

She eyed the extended hand, thinking of the mission

they'd just completed, the lives they'd saved. "There are still people to help, and bad guys to stop."

Eddie dropped his head and sighed. "Yes, Jules. That will continue to be the case for the next thousand years. I only meant that maybe you were up for rewarding your efforts now. Taking a few days off to recharge your batteries."

"But what about—"

"Fletcher can handle Ghost Squadron," Eddie interrupted.

Julianna looked around, like she was searching for an answer to this riddle Eddie was proposing. "What if Hatch needs our help with something?"

"He has Knox, and you know that if those two are working on something, they don't want us spying."

Julianna shook her head, her eyes distant in thought. "I'm just not sure if—"

Eddie turned, striding away. "Nevermind. I'll be in the lounge, if you're looking for me."

Julianna looked down at Harley, who gave her "that" look. She sighed. "Eddie, wait."

He halted, turned his chin over his shoulder, and regarded her with a serious look. "What?"

"I'm just not the vacationing type," she explained.

He pivoted, pointing at the dog at her heels. "You weren't the dog type before, either."

"It's just that vacations seem like something you do when there's been a happy ending, and I never want to delude myself into thinking the fight is over," Julianna explained.

Eddie strode over, a meaningful look on his face. "Vacations are what you do when you want to relax and spend time with someone, unobstructed by the distractions of everyday life."

"I like those distractions," Julianna argued, peering out the bay windows at stars that didn't have names.

Eddie laughed. "And I love that about you."

"You know I'm a workaholic who overdoes everything. I may never get my shit together and learn how to relax," Julianna admitted.

Eddie smiled. "I don't believe that for a minute. I'm the fuck-up, but do you know what we are together?"

Idiots, Pip offered.

Julianna shook her head. "What are we?"

"We're perfect," he said. "You keep me balanced, and I tell you when it's time to take a vacation. So what do you say, Jules? Ricky Bobby told me about a perfect place to unwind."

"He is good with picking destinations," Julianna said, allowing an excited smile.

"And this is not a happy ending," Eddie said, motioning between the two of them. "It's better. It's a happy beginning."

Once more, Eddie extended his hand to Julianna. This time she took it, allowing him to lead her away as the ship headed deep into space where the adventures were limitless.

THE END

Coming to the end of a series is always acidic syrup. Why yes, I did thesaurus the term "bitter sweet" because although it's inevitably what I mean, I didn't want to be cliché. Anyway, when I completed this book I was all like, "Yay! I finished my first space opera!" And at the same time, I was all, "No! Give me back my friends!" Please don't tell my "real" friends I said that or they'll again try to make me leave the house and have "authentic" interactions. So overrated.

Speaking of talking to real people. I did that recently. I found myself in a hotel bar. The reasons are inconsequential. A few of us lonely travelers were picking over our salads and pretending that eating at a bar with strangers wasn't weird. So one guy asks the lot of us, "What does everyone do?"

One guy said, "I'm an accountant." Everyone ignored that guy. *Who even let him in here?*

Another guy said he worked for a droid company. You

know I picked that guy's brain later for fodder. *And that's how you expense a dinner.*

Then after a few generic answers, I entered the convo. "I write sci-fi, fantasy space opera." And just like that I became the person of interests. You see, I already know that I have the coolest job. We've discussed that in the author notes before. But it was in that moment that I realized everyone else *also* thought I had the coolest job ever. Okay, more on strange convos I have with strangers later. Maybe in the next book.

Also, I was joking about the accountant. Some of my best friends are accountants.

Did I tell you all that I allow my 6-year-old to name pretty much whatever she wants in my books? It's a perk of the job. She's responsible for naming the snake race called the Saverus. I also asked her to name the utopian planet that Ricky Bobby takes the crew to in this book. Noircun may seem like a random string of letters and that's because it's unicorn rearranged. Bam! You never saw that one coming, right?

So the ark on Savern was a ton of fun to create. I can't take all the credit though. Again, I asked for inspiration from readers and they came through big time. The genius that had the idea for blood sucking humming birds was Kristoffer Pyle. Tracey Byrnes was the mastermind behind the vegetables that put Eddie to sleep. And not only did Lisa Frett offer up the name for the book, which won the popular vote on Facebook, but she also had lots of other brilliant ideas. For instance, that whole Pip and Eddie joyride in the car was one of her suggestions. Oh, and she'd mentioned something about a vegan craving chicken wings and I was like, say no more. I need all the opportunities I can get to make vegan jokes. I hope you all don't mind. I live in Southern California, right next to Malibu. Everyone here is too cool for school and have their H2O protein shakes at tea time while snacking on seaweed crumpets and talking about Pilates. I LOVE where I live, but man these people are weird. So this is my outlet. As an aside, one of my friends told me her husband was selling boot-legged whiskey to pay for her Pilates classes. I was like, I fucking love this place!

Why yes, I've digressed. Moving on. Nicole Emens was the smarty-pants who gave me the idea for the adorable creature who tried to bite Eddie's hand off. Love that. Lori Hendricks also encouraged me to finally bring Jules and Eddie together. She also offered up a lot of awesome ideas that I've thrown into many of the books. And it was Ron Gailey and Diane Brenner who gave me the ideas for the weapons. So good. Last, but never least it was Alastar Wilson who had the suggestion for the Corvette Stingray which Pip wrecks into a nuclear missile, because we go big or we go home.

I hope I'm not missing anyone, and I'm sure I am. Sorry. I'm so grateful for all the suggestions. You all really encourage me. Thank you to JIT for making each book better. I wished I could spend all day chatting with everyone on Facebook but then there would be no books.

Speaking of butterscotch and dimples, I'll turn you over to the guy you all came to see. Here's Michael-Fucking-Anderson.

Check out Sarah Noffke's Paranormal Thriller:

Ren Series:

Get it here

He is the most powerful man to ever live, and therefore doomed to misery.

Born with the power to control minds, hypnotize others, and read thoughts, Ren Lewis, is certain of one thing: God made a mistake. No one should be born with so much power. A monster awoke in him the same year he received his gifts.

At ten years old. A prepubescent boy with the ability to control others might merely abuse his powers, but Ren allowed it to corrupt him. And since he can have and do anything he wants, Ren should be happy. However, his journey teaches him that harboring so much power doesn't bring happiness, it steals it.

Once this realization sets in, Ren makes up his mind to do the one thing that can bring his tortured soul some peace. He must kill the monster.

Read <u>Ren: The Man Behind the Monster.</u>

AUTHOR NOTES - MICHAEL ANDERLE

WRITTEN MAY 15TH, 2018

Seriously, Noffke? *Anderson?*

So, first (or second, depending on how you look at things), THANK YOU for not only reading our stories, but reading all seven in this series, and *now* reading our *Author Notes* at the end!

Sarah is already working hard to the next adventures, and I am going to surprise her (eventually) with a logo for a coffee mug. (Editor's note: Um, MA, maybe not so much of a surprise now?) More on that in her next book!

Now I'm going to give you a little inside scoop and discuss another series we are working on.

More specifically, I'm going to tell you a bit about how collaborating with Sarah worked out to modify the angle of the series.

One of the interesting aspects of collaboration has to do with inspiration. We can often talk back and forth and go down various rabbit trails and holes until we come up with a concept we both like. Me, I often feel out what my collaborator likes and go from there.

Except with Sarah. Sarah's take makes it a bit different...because she likes the *bad guys.*

I know it takes a good bad guy to carry a story, but I'm kind of a good guy (or girl) type of author. I like to dream up neat protagonists we get to spend time with and go from there.

Sarah, on the other hand, likes to think of slavering teeth connected to bodies that turn your dreams go upside down and make you want to call your Mom although you're forty-eight.

Just kidding, I'm not forty-eight.

However, this time she was waxing poetic about a monster type and I was like 'huh?' then, "Hey, I have something to show you! Are you near your computer?"

She was.

If you have spent any time in our Kurtherian Gambit series, you have probably come across a monster or alien drawn by Eric Quigley.

Eric is responsible for making my lazy alien descriptions come alive.

A long time ago (well, "long" in Indie Publishing Time, or IPT), Eric was messing around with some drawings for LARGE aliens...and I wanted them. They weren't based on any of my descriptions, but I liked them and I could afford to purchase four (4) of them and hold them "for later."

But later never came.

Except...now I pulled them up on the computer and

sent them to my monster-loving collaborator to see what she thought of them.

And of course, our little Eat the Humans loved them all!

We spit-balled concepts back and forth for a series that might include LARGE-ASSED MONSTERS (LAMs)—or I guess they could be LARGE-ASSED ALIENS (LAAs)—and be (for me) a lot of fun.

It took us about fourteen minutes to hammer out the bones of the idea, and we are pretty damned excited to move the series along. Unfortunately, it won't be out in a few weeks like most of our efforts, since we have the afore-mentioned AOE series starting up soon.

But we WILL get to it…I promise!

Now, back to Michael-fucking-Anderson…

Sarah and I were talking a little yesterday about this new series and she mentioned that she was going to give me a softball toss to help me with my author notes.

How nice that the softball toss was a purposeful mistake with my last name.

There goes the branding.

Here I could say something about Sarah's (very) slow slide down the slippery slope of her mental faculties for making such a simple mistake (but I won't.) Or I could discuss my last name as being easily mistaken (it usually isn't, believe it or not.)

What I *will* say is that I find my collaborator too damned nice to say anything ugly and leave it at that.

<Sigh—where's a good feeling of righteous indignation when you need one?>

When Sarah and I spoke a couple of months ago, she told me the story that if we die without sharing that song, that music, that story in our mind, then it dies with us. I still think about that to this day.

Because of that little story—and a lot of time thinking about stories dying with us—LMBPN Publishing (my company) is going to do something pretty *DAMNED* ballsy for a small indie publishing house.

We are going to try and hit four hundred (400!) book releases in 2019.

Four Hundred!

To give this number some context, that is a release every day of the year plus a few more.

There are the "Big Four" trad pub houses, and I believe the fifth largest is Kensington (family-owned) and they have been around for decades (since the 70s, maybe?)

I read yesterday that all five publish seven hundred (700) stories a year.

LMBPN is just two and a half years old, and if we come close to hitting four hundred books in 2019 we will be in the *top five percent of all fiction publishing companies* (I believe).

Whether we make it, or not, I'm very proud to know that Sarah will be with us, trying like hell to help us hit our numbers!

Please join us in our quest and see just how many LMPBN books YOU can read, and perhaps we will have Jeff Bezos asking…

"Who the HELL is LMBPN Publishing?"

Ad Aeternitatem,

Michael ~~Anderson~~ Anderle

ACKNOWLEDGMENTS

Sarah Noffke

Thank you to Michael Anderle for taking my calls and allowing me to play in this universe. It's been a blast since the beginning.

Thank you to Craig Martelle for cheering for me. I've learned so much working with you. This wild ride just keeps going and going.

Thank you to Jen, Tim, Steve, Andrew and Jeff for all the work on the books, covers and championing so much of the publishing.

Thank you to our beta team. I can't believe how fast you all can turn around books. The JIT team sometimes scares me, but usually just with how impressively knowledgeable they are.

Thank you to our amazing readers. I asked myself a question the other day and it had a strange answer. I asked if I would still write if trapped on a desert island and no one would ever read the books. The answer was yes, but the feeling connected to it was different. It wouldn't be as much fun to write if there wasn't awesome readers to share it with. Thank you.

Thank you to my friends and family for all the support and love.

Sarah Noffke, an Amazon Best Seller, writes YA and NA sci-fi fantasy, paranormal and urban fantasy. She is the author of the Lucidites, Reverians, Ren, Vagabond Circus, Olento Research and Soul Stone Mage series. Noffke holds a Masters of Management and teaches college business courses. Most of her students have no idea that she toils away her hours crafting fictional characters. Noffke's books are top rated and best-sellers on Kindle. Currently, she has eighteen novels published. Her books are available in paperback, audio and in Spanish, Portuguese and Italian. http://www.sarahnoffke.com

Check out other work by this author <u>here.</u>

The Soul Stone Mage Series:
<u>**House of Enchanted #1:**</u>
The Kingdom of Virgo has lived in peace for thousands of years...until now.

The humans from Terran have always been real

assholes to the witches of Virgo. Now a silent war is brewing, and the timing couldn't be worse. Princess Azure will soon be crowned queen of the Kingdom of Virgo.

In the Dark Forest a powerful potion-maker has been murdered.

Charmsgood was the only wizard who could stop a deadly virus plaguing Virgo. He also knew about the devastation the people from Terran had done to the forest.

Azure must protect her people. Mend the Dark Forest. Create alliances with savage beasts. No biggie, right?

But on coronation day everything changes. Princess Azure isn't who she thought she was and that's a big freaking problem.

Welcome to The Revelations of Oriceran. Check out the entire series here.

The Lucidites Series:

Awoken, #1:

Around the world humans are hallucinating after sleepless nights.

In a sterile, underground institute the forecasters keep reporting the same events.

And in the backwoods of Texas, a sixteen-year-old girl is about to be caught up in a fierce, ethereal battle.

Meet Roya Stark. She drowns every night in her dreams, spends her hours reading classic literature to avoid her family's ridicule, and is prone to premonitions—which are becoming more frequent. And now her dreams are filled with strangers offering to reveal what she has always wanted to know: Who is she? That's the question that haunts her, and she's about to find out. But will Roya live to regret learning the truth?

Stunned, #2

Revived, #3

The Reverians Series:

Defects, #1:

In the happy, clean community of Austin Valley, everything appears to be perfect. Seventeen-year-old Em Fuller, however, fears something is askew. Em is one of the new generation of Dream Travelers. For some reason, the gods have not seen fit to gift all of them with their expected special abilities. Em is a Defect—one of the unfortunate Dream Travelers not gifted with a psychic power. Desperate to do whatever it takes to earn her gift, she endures painful daily injections along with commands from her overbearing, loveless father. One of the few bright spots in her life is the return of a friend she had thought dead—but with his return comes the knowledge of a shocking, unforgivable truth. The society Em thought was protecting her has actually been betraying her, but she has no idea how to break away from its authority without hurting everyone she loves.

Rebels, #2

Warriors, #3

Vagabond Circus Series:

Suspended, #1:

When a stranger joins the cast of Vagabond Circus—a circus that is run by Dream Travelers and features real

BOOKS BY SARAH NOFFKE

magic—mysterious events start happening. The once orderly grounds of the circus become riddled with hidden threats. And the ringmaster realizes not only are his circus and its magic at risk, but also his very life.

Vagabond Circus caters to the skeptics. Without skeptics, it would close its doors. This is because Vagabond Circus runs for two reasons and only two reasons: first and foremost to provide the lost and lonely Dream Travelers a place to be illustrious. And secondly, to show the nonbelievers that there's still magic in the world. If they believe, then they care, and if they care, then they don't destroy. They stop the small abuse that day-by-day breaks down humanity's spirit. If Vagabond Circus makes one skeptic believe in magic, then they halt the cycle, just a little bit. They allow a little more love into this world. That's Dr. Dave Raydon's mission. And that's why this ringmaster recruits. That's why he directs. That's why he puts on a show that makes people question their beliefs. He wants the world to believe in magic once again.

Paralyzed, #2
Released, #3

Ren Series:
Ren: The Man Behind the Monster, #1:
Born with the power to control minds, hypnotize others, and read thoughts, Ren Lewis, is certain of one thing: God made a mistake. No one should be born with so much power. A monster awoke in him the same year he received his gifts. At ten years old. A prepubescent boy with the ability to control others might merely abuse his

268

powers, but Ren allowed it to corrupt him. And since he can have and do anything he wants, Ren should be happy. However, his journey teaches him that harboring so much power doesn't bring happiness, it steals it. Once this realization sets in, Ren makes up his mind to do the one thing that can bring his tortured soul some peace. He must kill the monster.

Note This book is NA and has strong language, violence and sexual references.

Ren: God's Little Monster, #2
Ren: The Monster Inside the Monster, #3
Ren: The Monster's Adventure, #3.5
Ren: The Monster's Death

Olento Research Series:
Alpha Wolf, #1:
Twelve men went missing.

Six months later they awake from drug-induced stupors to find themselves locked in a lab.

And on the night of a new moon, eleven of those men, possessed by new—and inhuman—powers, break out of their prison and race through the streets of Los Angeles until they disappear one by one into the night.

Olento Research wants its experiments back. Its CEO, Mika Lenna, will tear every city apart until he has his werewolves imprisoned once again. He didn't undertake a huge risk just to lose his would-be assassins.

However, the Lucidite Institute's main mission is to save the world from injustices. Now, it's Adelaide's job to find these mutated men and protect them and society, and fast. Already around the nation, wolflike men are being spotted. Attacks on innocent women are happening. And then, Adelaide realizes what her next step must be: She has to find the alpha wolf first. Only once she's located him can she stop whoever is behind this experiment to create wild beasts out of human beings.

Lone Wolf, #2
    Rabid Wolf, #3
    Bad Wolf, #4

CONNECT WITH THE AUTHORS

Michael Anderle Social

Website:
http://kurtherianbooks.com/

Email List:
http://kurtherianbooks.com/email-list/

Facebook Here:
https://www.
facebook.com/TheKurtherianGambitBooks/